Par

WATER PUP

written and illustrated by
Peter Parnall

Macmillan Publishing Company   New York

Maxwell Macmillan Canada   Toronto

Maxwell Macmillan International
New York   Oxford   Singapore   Sydney

Macmillan Publishing Company is part of the
Maxwell Communication Group of Companies.
Macmillan Publishing Company
866 Third Avenue, New York, NY 10022
Maxwell Macmillan Canada, Inc.
1200 Eglinton Avenue East, Suite 200
Don Mills, Ontario M3C 3N1
First edition
Printed in the United States of America

10 9 8 7 6 5 4 3 2 1

The text of this book is set in 11 point Primer.
The illustrations are rendered in pen and ink.

Parnall, Peter.
    Water pup / written and illustrated by Peter Parnall. — 1st ed.
        p.   cm.
    Summary: Lop, a gentle part-Labrador puppy born in the wild, loses her mother, learns to hunt and to survive the dangers of nature, is raised by a fox, and eventually finds a home with humans.
    ISBN 0-02-770151-4
    1. Dogs—Juvenile fiction. [1. Dogs—Fiction.] I. Title.
PZ10.3.P228Wat 1993   [Fic]—dc20   92-40850

For Teenie P.

WATER PUP

Prologue

The air was very still.

Raven was still as well. He perched on the tallest dead stub of a boundary pine at the edge of a large field, watching.

Nothing moved.

No blade of brittle timothy grass swayed, and the dried cones of a sea of black-eyed Susans were still, just waiting for the wind to dance and help them spread their seed.

Near the center of the field lay a large pond. It nestled in a natural basin and was fed by runoff from the surrounding land and five small springs that welled up though the blue clay at its southern end.

Raven's end.

Throughout the year, except when ice sealed the view, Raven came. He came in the late afternoon, for he knew about reflections. He knew that when the sun fell behind the pines that bordered the field's western edge he did not see clouds or dancing light on the surface of the pond, he saw the bottom. He saw the bottom in the shallows, around the edges, where tadpoles, frogs, and minnows lived . . . and sometimes made mistakes.

Raven's aim was to take advantage of mistakes.

But on this warm, quiet September afternoon he was, for the moment, content to sit and watch.

Four or five feet from the edge of the pond, where lily pads grew in deeper water, he could see young leaves that had not quite reached the surface. They had flattened out in anticipation of their final position barely inches away, and some late-hatching tadpoles rested upon them. Sometimes they fed on the algae that had already begun to form, sometimes . . . sometimes . . . they just rested.

No wind marred the surface of the water. No reflections. No ripples of light. The underwater leaves and their soft little hitchhikers seemed to float in midair.

Raven watched.

Others watched, as well.

Mouse and his brethren waited and watched for shadows to lengthen before venturing forth in search of an evening meal. Heron watched Bass, and from his lair beneath the cover of pickerel weed an old frog waited for mayflies to hover within reach of his sticky tongue. Two feathered jewels watched from high in the safety of a thistle plant. Goldfinches. They watched a mother fox teaching her three fat pups the art of catching crickets.

This was September. Cricket month.

Raven's attention was so taken by the activity of the cricket hunters that he hadn't noticed another who had entered the scene.

Halfway back up the family's route into the field lay a fourth pup. A yellowish tan. She was larger than the others, and her ears were different. One hung down, and the other looked as though it wanted to stand up, but it folded a bit, and pointed to the side. There were shadows between her ribs. She was lean, and her coat did not shine like the fur of the roly-poly cricket-eaters.

The thin puppy had been observing the fox family for some time. She had seen them several hours earlier, when they were walking down a logging road near Raven's nighttime roost. At first she had wanted to run to them, for she sensed a kinship with the foxes, and she wanted desperately to share it. But something made her hang back.

The lop-eared puppy followed the family at a distance. The mother was aware of Lop's presence, and at one point, when her pups were strung out too far behind and she thought the ungainly puppy had ventured too close, she bared her teeth. After that, her own pups stayed close to her side.

The family unit was familiar to Lop, and the sight of it prompted an empty feeling in her heart. A loneliness. She missed her mother and brothers. She remembered the warmth, the fun, the good food that were always there.

Mostly she remembered her mother.

Chapter One

Late May—a cool, drizzly night. Too cool for mosquitoes to be searching for their first blood meal, but not so for blackflies. They had been emerging from their watery nurseries with a vengeance.

Cool, warm, sun or moon, they swarmed, drawing energy from anything warm that moved. Their bites drove even Moose to distraction, and Raccoon. Deer sought the protection of dense fir growth, but no one could escape the pesky flies.

An old dog stood by the side of a lonely country road, hardly noticing the tiny insects that attacked her nose. Her gaze was fixed in the direction she had last seen car lights. *Her* car lights.

She was a yellow-colored dog. Her mother had been a yellow Lab, and her father was a mongrel of particularly fine parentage. Royalty of sorts. *His* father had been a malamute who had seen the center of many show rings, and his mother had been a bull terrier. She had not only been shown throughout her life, but had walked away with just about every blue ribbon her owners went after. They were more than a little angry when she got out one night and visited her malamute friend next door.

The old dog began to shiver. The light rain had begun to penetrate her fur, for she had not inherited the dense undercoat of her long-haired grandfather. Her gaze never wavered from the pavement where it disappeared into the night, and she did not understand. She expected her people to return. The minutes dragged by, then an hour passed.

She did not understand.

An emptiness began to creep into her heart. It joined the wet in her fur and the confusion that was beginning to overtake her.

She did not want to stray. Something *told* her not to stray, but after almost two hours standing in the rain she began slowly walking along the side of the road toward where her car lights had disappeared.

Dog was not large. She weighed perhaps sixty pounds. She was quite old, however, fourteen in fact, and had given birth to eleven litters of puppies during those fourteen years.

This night she walked as an old dog would, with short carefully placed steps. It was very dark, and she was trying to see down the road, while at the same time avoiding the numerous sharp stones along its edge. The rain and a heavy heart weighed her down as she made her way slowly through the dark.

An added weight made her anxious. For within her were six heavy puppies very close to being born.

Drizzle turned to rain. Then wind entered cruelly into the night and began to drive wetness against the lay of her fur. Discomfort overtook confusion, and in the manner of her less domestic ancestors, Dog's instinct for survival quickened her pace. Those within her womb kicked and rolled as the unsteadiness of her gait broadcast a change in the condition of their world.

Somehow they sensed an urgency, for the blood that coursed through their mother's veins instilled in them new instincts, too, no matter how unrefined.

Warmth . . . safety.

Human words, but instinctive desires that contribute to survival on cold, rainy nights.

"Hurry."

The old dog had gone just a little way when she heard a faint motor sound. She wasn't sure of it at first, but each gust of wind brought it a bit closer. Dog stopped, turned, and strained to see through the sheets of rain.

Then lights—she saw headlights approaching, and her heart beat faster. They had come back! A sense of relief flowed over her, for now the rain didn't matter, the cold did not matter, she could concentrate only on the approaching lights and their promise of warmth and safety. Her tongue lolled to the side and her heart was full, as she anticipated the comfort of a warm car seat.

But the car did not slow down. It sped past her, and over the roar of the engine she heard,

"Damn dog!"

Her heart fell once again as this new set of red taillights disappeared through the rain.

Bewildered, Dog looked woodenly down the road in each direction, then turned and moved one foot in front of the other until the repeated motion seemed to have some purpose. She was totally soaked now, not only with

rain, but with salty water from the road that the car tires had sprayed over her as it passed.

The old dog plodded on for almost an hour, occasionally looked to the side in some hope of finding shelter. Thick spruce and fir trees lined the road. With the visibility so restricted by darkness and rain, the trees seemed to be an impenetrable wall. Then she saw a light.

She stopped.

To her right was a wide gap in the barrier of trees. A driveway. A hundred feet or so away stood the faint bulk of a small building with a tiny light showing faintly through a window.

She watched for a moment and listened.

No sounds. Nothing. She walked slowly forward, trying to hear for sounds through the rain. The old dog had no way of knowing it, but this was the first indication of caution that had ever entered her life. She had always trusted, trusted unfailingly. But now, abandoned and alone, confusion began to overtake her. Doubts entered her old heart, and she listened. She watched.

Still no sounds.

The building she had discovered was a weekend camp, perhaps a summer camp. The people who owned it had returned to the city after spending a weekend fixing the place up. They had taken window boards down, cut wood, found all the mouse nests left over from the migration many rodents make into buildings in their effort to escape the winter snows. The light that glowed faintly through the window was just a night-light, left on to discourage petty thieves.

Dog walked carefully around the cabin, exploring all four sides. The building was situated on an uneven piece of ground and had a crawl space beneath. Along the rear wall a small opening gave access to pipes and a storage area. She then walked up stairs that led to a door, sniffed the threshold, and found it had not been too long since another dog had passed through that door. She still heard no sounds.

Satisfied that no dangers lurked, she descended the stairs, walked around to the back of the building, and cautiously entered the crawl space. There needed to be no great comforts there, for just to be out of the driving rain was comfort enough. Among the scraps of wood and other assorted junk she found a large depression in the dirt, where the phantom dog of the threshold had lain to cool himself from the previous summer's heat. The dirt was loose and dry.

She circled several times before lowering herself carefully into the powdery nest. The water that soaked Dog's fur dripped onto the ground around her, forming a circle of little, muddy gobs, and though her back was wet and cold, the trapped body heat beneath began to win the battle.

The unborn puppies had been quiet during the last of Dog's journey up the road, making no movement at all. She had been thoroughly distracted by the wind, rain, and cold. She had not noticed.

Now, though sleep demanded to overtake her, she fought it, uneasy over the lack of movement in her belly. The old dog fought to keep her lids from drooping as she watched the rain slowly slacken and become a gentle drizzle. Wind subsided, too, so pines and firs no longer moaned.

She listened. There were only whispers now.

Then Dog felt someone within her do a barrel roll, and she knew all was well.

She slept.

Blackfly and friends appeared the following day. A sunny day, and warm—and here they had a nice, fat nose on which to feast! And they did.

Dog awoke slowly. Her coat was dry, but her muscles ached and she was loath to move. Her pups had become more active during the night and now seemed to be moving inside her with ever-increasing vigor. The tenacious little flies feeding upon her nose could not be ignored, and when she tried to brush them off with a forepaw she felt soreness in the muscles of her shoulder. When she opened her eyes and peered outside, she saw the promise of a warmer day. And she felt hunger begin to gnaw.

Something else, something in the way her pups were acting today, made her more alert. She rose slowly to her feet, walked out from under the building into the new day, and headed down the drive.

Hungry.

Move out.

When Dog came to the edge of the road she turned right and headed in the same direction she had taken the night before. The brightness of the morning had a positive effect, and though she still had remnants of confusion running through her brain and soreness in her joints, she stepped along at a livelier pace.

Hungry. Hungry.

Hungry.

And hurry. She could not ask, "Hurry, for what?" But instinct knew.

Dog carried on along the road for over a mile. She saw beer cans here and there, discarded by ignorant folk with no regard. Perhaps a can covered the spot where a black-eyed Susan might have grown, further on, in July. Here and there old wrappers lay, and a bag of trash that had fallen from a truck on the way to the dump.

Another quarter mile and she stopped, her nose lifted to the breeze.

An interesting smell. She knew that smell. A few yards farther down the roadside she came upon a crumpled paper bag. It was on its side, partially ripped, and the contents showed clearly as Dog lowered her head to investigate. Two Styrofoam cups, one with a rip, some napkins and wrappers, and . . . and . . . a half-eaten roll and a small piece of meat. The remains of a burger (at least the modern version of one). She pawed at the bag in a tentative way, and the roll fell out.

She picked up the roll but didn't bolt it down as most dogs would. She chewed it to mush, savoring the flavor before swallowing. Next, the meat. Dog chewed that carefully, too. She nosed the bag in case any treat remained, but there were only smells. A meager meal, but enough to ease her hunger and let her focus clearly on a more urgent task.

The old dog resumed her journey to somewhere, along the side of the road. As she traveled, her gaze scanned the edges for possible treats, but there were no more.

She was thirsty, too. But the few puddles she found were too salty. They would be until many rains washed the last road salt to the side and into the ground. It killed some plants, and nourished others. Mouse knew. He liked salty leaves, and spent time at night by the side of the road.

Screech Owl knew that. He hunted the roadsides almost every night. He liked Mouse.

The day wore on. In spite of sun, a snack, and a fair-weather day, fatigue began to drain the overburdened dog.

Shadows lengthened.

A coolness was in the air now, and she knew well the dangers of waiting too long to find shelter. Cars, familiar faces, and man-made comforts were not her quarry now. It was more simple: warm . . . and dry.

Food could wait. She wanted warm . . . and dry.

Dog came to a point on the side of the road where there stood a very large rock. Beside this rock was a wide path. Not a driveway, but a rough path, big enough for a large vehicle to pass. It had been made over 150 years before by a son of the German immigrant who had settled this land. He used it to haul logs from the woods with oxen.

The wide path beckoned. Certainly the roadside promised no shelters at all.

She crossed.

A few yards from the paved road the logging path emerged from the trees and wound its way through a small field dotted with the seedlings of pine, fir, and birch, the offspring of those giants along the borders. The field had not been mown for half a dozen years, and if not done within the next few, would be well on its way to becoming forest again.

To her right was a gnarled apple tree. It was hollow and dying, but had sent up a shoot that was over six feet high and promised to carry on the tradition of bearing fine greening apples that would supply a generation or two, or three, or four, with unlimited apple pies.

A hundred yards beyond the apple tree, the road led into tall pine woods.

Dog followed it.

The woods were beginning to darken, and as the path went on it led to a small patch of birch woods. They were brighter. The setting sun reflected off a passing cloud and filled the delicate birches with light, and Dog turned toward the more optimistic scene.

Another logging trail led her way.

She followed that for fifty yards until she stood before a huge outcropping of granite ledge.

The tired old dog stared at it for a moment, examining its western face. From the top of the rock exploded the loud snort of a startled deer. Dog tensed, ready to flee. She had never heard this noise before. She was a city dog.

The deer walked to the edge of the rock, tail up, ears a-cock and ready to run.

He saw Dog.

It didn't *look* like a coyote.

But it smelled like one.

He turned tail and bounced down the other side of the ledge, and with every other stride blasted forth a warning snort, telling all within earshot that danger lurked nearby.

Little did Deer know that the old female dog was so exhausted that she could not have been a threat to anything that was capable of movement.

As soon as his tail bounced out of sight and she could no longer hear his snorts, Dog relaxed and returned her attention the rock.

There was a large fissure in its face, a crack about four feet off the ground, and its lower edge formed a ledge.

It slanted slightly toward the ground, and as she walked to it she could see a cavity within. Laboriously Dog made her way to the lower edge, got a foothold, and hauled herself upon it. The ledge was just wide enough for her to make her way along without falling off. Midway along the ledge, the crack became large enough for her to squeeze into, and she did.

There were many unfamiliar smells there. Animal smells. She knew none of them, but she did know they were not fresh, and she was not afraid. The space widened and became a tiny cavern. Within it were the punky remains of unrecognizable vegetable matter and some small deposits of bones, the whole forming a bedding that would have been hard to improve upon had it been arranged on purpose.

She turned and faced the opening. The birch woods were beginning to darken now.

This was a safe place. A dry place. Animals just know such things.

The tired old dog did several preparatory turns, in the fashion of her wild ancestors, lay down, and slept. No blackfly could have kept her awake this night. Not blackfly, not hunger, not fear, not even the remains of a broken heart.

Chapter Two

Deep within the rocky den, sometime during the night, six tiny puppies squeezed their way into the world. By the time a tentative ray of light worked its way through to the birth chamber, all six had squirmed their way into position and were nursing contentedly.

The old dog lay on her side, every now and then raising her head to look at the marvelous thing she had done.

She had borne many puppies. Many. But each time it seemed like something new. Each time it was almost as if she were renewed as well.

But this was different.

The litters of her past had been born into a sheltered life. One with a roof. One where bowls of food were presented at least once a day.

This was different.

She was old. She had far less milk than before, and the pups soon depleted her supply. It would replenish soon enough, but not as bountifully as in years past.

Dog didn't know these things, of course. She was content for the moment, and as the puppies snoozed soundly after their first meal she examined them closely, licking clean whatever she had missed when they were born. Five were males. They were all the same size. They were the most active squirmers, the first to attach to a nipple, and the loudest when voicing a complaint. Loudest? Louder than whom?

Louder than the sixth.

A female. She was much smaller than her brothers, and a different color to boot. They were a grizzly, black-gray color. They resembled their malamute great-grandfather when he had been born. This tiny girl puppy was yellowish tan, and looked like her grandmother, the yellow Lab. But she was not as large at birth as her grandma had been, and if there was a squirming match at feeding time, she often got pushed aside.

Dog was proud of them all. The female pup stood out from the rest, so she was usually the first to feel the comforting strokes of her mother's tongue.

That first day was spent sleeping, cleaning, squirming, and feeling pleased. Dog felt hunger, but her overwhelming emotion was one of satisfaction and pride in her new family.

During the times that the puppies slept, she listened to the sounds of the surrounding woods. It was a quiet, sunny day with little wind, just enough to mask the body warmth that slowly leaked from the entrance to the den. There was no warm, airborne path for blackflies to follow, so it was a bug-free day.

She heard Moose when he walked through the shallow pond that lay beyond, on the edge of the birches. He was hoping for a meal of succulents that grew there later in the year. He was too early.

She heard the high-pitched *Scree-e-e-e* of a broad-winged hawk as he soared overhead, trying hopefully to lure a mate. The ones he had wooed the year before had already chosen, and were now building their nests. He was too late.

She heard the croak of Heron as she flew overhead on her way to a day's fishing, and she heard the creak of Raven's wings. This noise puzzled the old lady dog. It sounded like a man-made thing gone awry, not an animal noise at all.

In the afternoon a red squirrel came to call—came to call on a secret hoard of seeds he had buried in the den the autumn before. Dog did not hear him at first. Out of the corner of her eye she saw something . . . flick!

She turned her head and saw Squirrel, crouched, silhouetted against the bright light at the opening of the den.

Agitated Squirrel. He flicked and twitched his tail several times, giving accent to the spark in his eye. His little head jerked up, then down, and he vanished. From halfway up a slim birch trunk he launched forth with a scolding chatter, telling everyone within earshot that something new was afoot.

He, Squirrel, had been wronged again, chatter, chatter. Chatter and squeak, his world was a shambles! Dog and her puppies were nesting on top of his evening meal!

Once convinced the tirade was to no effect, Squirrel hopped off toward another hoard.

Night approached once again. The view outside began to gray. The mother dog crept close to the hole and listened. Peeper frogs were beginning to peep, and soon green frogs joined in. Dog knew of frogs. She had eaten one once. She stole it from the cat next door.

That cat, it seemed, almost *lived* on frogs. At least, in the spring of the year, when they were all around. One day she entered Dog's yard with a bullfrog she'd caught, too big to finish all at once, and the dog simply took it.

They were friends. The cat didn't object. And Dog enjoyed eating the treat. A treat. It *was* a treat.

Now the complaint in her belly and the sound of the frogs nearby urged her to think there was a meal out there, near where Moose had walked.

The thought made her tongue wet. She dripped a delicate drool, then crept back to her pups to give them one last pull at what was left of her milk before setting out on an evening hunt for frogs.

Frog, had he been a storybook frog, would have felt lucky, and would have had a big smile on his face. Moose had walked by earlier in the day, when the little green frog was resting by the edge of the tiny pond, under two overlapping birch leaves. They had dried and dropped the fall before, but had not gone to ground. A mass of drying ferns blocked their way, and it was only when snows weighed down the ferns that the two leaves reached their final resting place.

Now the ferns were coming to life again, and the first shoot had propped up the leaves just enough. Just enough to provide Frog with a perfect lean-to. A perfect little roof.

Moose was unaware of Frog as he strode forth into the water. He wouldn't have cared anyway. He left a deep footprint in the muck less than a half inch from where the little amphibian crouched, and water quickly oozed forth, filling it to the brim.

But Frog was *not* a storybook frog. He did not smile. He did not anticipate future events. What he *did* do was eat heartily one evening when the eggs that Mosquito laid in the water of the moose-print finally emerged into view as adult mosquitoes.

Frog managed to catch them all.

Dog carefully picked her way between clumps of suckers that grew from small maple stumps, left when the birch woods had been weeded two years before. They had begun to leaf out, and provided good cover for any clever hunter.

The old dog was a city girl, however, not a born stalker. She picked her way carefully, not to make her advance more stealthy, but simply to stay on her feet! At age fourteen her athletic days were long over, but she had a good eye, and she had a great nose.

Standing close to Frog's leaf roof, Dog could tell Moose had been there, and when the light breeze shifted she could also tell that Deer was somewhere close. She didn't know who Moose was, but the first sight of Deer was still clear in her memory.

As the dog approached the water's edge, Frog heard her coming. He saw some cousins leap for safety from more exposed lookouts, then stick their eyes up, just above the water's surface, the better to examine Dog. She saw them jump, too late, of course. She could never move quickly enough to pounce on a frog that crouched so close to water. Somehow she knew that.

But she also knew about water. She loved to swim, and over the years had spent hundreds of hours swimming, diving, retrieving, and playing in lakes and ponds, in streams, and even in ocean surf a number of times, when her people had gone to the beach. She sensed she was no match for the quickness of frogs. But water-dog blood ran in her veins, Labrador blood. She stepped delicately over some budding ferns, and carefully, slowly, entered the pond. The bottom was soft with rotting leaves and slippery clay. She stood for a moment belly deep, then launched herself quietly, barely causing a ripple.

Frog watched her go, and he saw his cousins' eyes pop below the surface as Dog swam slowly by.

As she neared the opposite shore, Dog slowed, felt for the bottom, and stopped. Almost suspended, her toes barely touching, she examined the water's edge carefully. Next to a small rock sat a small green frog. Under a fallen branch was a leopard frog. He was a little farther back from shore, and was turned sideways. In the water to the right hung three sets of bulbous eyes. They seemed not to realize something was up, for they drifted . . . closer.

Dog breathed slower. Something inherited from wilder kin said, "Don't move. Quiet."

She did not move.

A gentle breeze brought the three drifting frogs closer, closer.

The old yellow head did not move.

One of the frogs touched her nose with the fingers of its right front foot, as if to steady itself in the breeze. Then the left foot reached out.

With an explosive move Dog flicked her nose. She caught the frog while it was still in flight, as she had done in the past with popcorn treats!

The other two floaters vanished at once, and several on shore disappeared as well. But Leopard Frog jumped farther up toward the woods. He felt safe there, for he

was swift on land, and had escaped great dangers a number of times.

The success of her catch encouraged the dog. She looked for the others, but they had hidden well.

All except Leopard Frog.

She walked slowly out of the water toward him.

Water dripped from her fur, and her udders swayed slightly as she took each step. The frog seemed unafraid. He had no knowledge of what had happened, had only witnessed a splash. Slow, dripping, yellow beasts were beyond his experience.

But she kept coming closer.

His little brain finally registered unease, or whatever happens to frogs when it's time to say,

"Uh-oh!"

He hopped three times, then hid in the base of a rotten trunk.

Dog did not run. The ground was too rough. But she saw where Leopard Frog hid.

Putting her muzzle in the opening, she cut off his escape. The desperate frog jumped and jumped and jumped. Each time he hit the ceiling of the small, punky cave he fell back and hit Dog's nose.

She then lay on her side.

The next time Frog jumped he fell to his death between open jaws, fuel for the milk factory that licked her lips. Frog gave his life for six puppies who waited in a rocky den. His life was not wasted.

The spark of fear and the loneliness that flowed through the old dog were tempered by the success of this first froggy meal. She had hunted, she had eaten, and she knew the little pond and its shores held many more meals.

It was almost dark now. She picked her way back to the big rock, climbed to the den, and was greeted by a bundle of mewing, wiggly, warm puppies.

Safe puppies.

During the next three months Dog became quite expert as a frog catcher. She tested the tastes of various insects, lucked upon and caught an occasional mouse or vole, and found ribbon snakes numerous, easy to catch, and quite good. They smelled a bit less than wonderful, but the meat was tasty. As the pups grew and began demanding more than milk, offerings of snakes and frogs made up the bulk of their diet.

Ordinarily the larger of the puppies would be the most successful at feeding time. When prey was delivered to the den, however, as often as not it was offered first to the little female, Lop. She had developed a more vigorous personality than her brothers and was usually in front, nearest the den opening, when her mother arrived home. Even if the pups were asleep at the back of the den, Dog always picked out Lop first, because of her yellow color.

They had color in common, and the pup had one ear similiar to her mother's—a Labrador ear. The other ear was in a constant state of indecision, and couldn't decide whether to be a Labrador ear or a malamute ear. It settled halfway in between, and hung out to the side. That was the one her brothers most often grabbed during a wrestling match. Any girl puppy who has to contend with five burly brothers either gets steamrolled or develops ways to outwit them. Lop found out quite by accident that one way to slow them up was to look and sound ferocious. It *had* to be an accident, for in her heart she was the most gentle one of all.

One afternoon Lop was near the entrance, waiting for

her mother to return from hunting, and the boys were horsing around on a large, flat ledge inside the den. The ledge was elevated, and there were several large, semiflat stones up there. Just as Dog came into view the puppies dislodged one of those stones, and when it fell, one of its sharp corners caught Lop directly on her tail!

She whirled around and let out a snarly screech that sent the others into shock. They tumbled off the ledge, scrambled to the rear of the den, and regarded her with disbelief. Ten pointy ears and ten wide eyes surrounded by fur watched.

They just watched.

When Dog entered with a large bullfrog in her jaws Lop sniffed it; then, hearing movement behind her, she turned quickly toward the advancing brothers. They tumbled back into a furry, protective pile again, probably expecting another awful noise.

There was none. But sister Lop had learned a lesson. A quick movement, especially when accompanied by a sharp voice, produced results: She ate that whole bullfrog herself. From then on, she ate *lots* of what her mom brought home, herself.

Dog's hunting trips took her farther and farther from the den site as the days wore on. The first bullfrog she brought home came from the pond in the field. Raven's pond. She became more expert at stalking her prey, and so began to deplete the supply of frogs that lived there. It had taken but a few days to eliminate them all from the little pond in the birches.

Drawn to the larger pond by the familiar evening music of frog songs, she discovered the much larger bullfrogs, and successfully stalked them. One small bullfrog was

33

the equal of six or eight of the green frogs she was used to catching, so far less effort was needed to supply her little family with adequate amounts of food.

Her trips to the field required covering more ground, and provided more accidental meetings with mice and snakes. They were slow, and easy to catch.

Up to this point the puppies had obediently stayed inside the den while their mother was away. The pups of wolves and foxes do the same, at first. But as the weather warms and the sun makes the woods a friendlier place, the young relish adventures outdoors, and play near the entrance to their dens. They wrestle about close by, and as they become more at ease with the surroundings they can often be seen napping, right out in the open. Lop took adventure a bit further.

She had often watched from the ledge as her mother went to the little pond to catch frogs, and was curious about the splashes created as Dog flipped frog after frog into the air.

And Lop was bold.

One morning after her mother had left, Lop climbed carefully off the ledge. Her brothers crowded the den entrance behind her, and one whined softly. She turned quickly, and he didn't whine again. The puppy picked her way carefully through the undergrowth as she had seen her mother do, and as she rounded a leafy clump of birch shoots a leopard frog jumped directly ahead of her! Lop jerked her head back in surprise. She had never seen a *live* frog before.

At first she wanted to play, and chased the frog. It jumped four or five times, and once she actually touched it with her paw, pinning his hind foot to the ground. He wriggled free and jumped again, making no attempt at finding cover.

Lop became aware of his smell. Some of it was on her paw, and now the game was over.

This was food.

She stepped slowly toward him, put her right paw carefully on the ground, then started to raise her left one. As she did so the spotted frog leaped, and before he hit the ground Lop was in motion. He barely had time to launch himself again before she was almost upon him. But he did.

She had a roly-poly, uncoordinated gait, accented by the uneven ground, but her persistence was enough to disorient the panicked frog. She finally pinned him with both front paws and watched him for a moment. He blinked his eyes repeatedly, sinking them partially into his head each time, and his throat pulsed rapidly. He appeared to be a frog with a lot of jumps left in him. She didn't want to play now.

She ate him.

With her first independent meal, Lop became more a part of the landscape than her brothers, more of a wild thing. Something magical had happened to her. She was no longer totally tied to them, or even to her mother, though the change was still very small. She still suckled along with her brothers for what little of her mother's milk still flowed. She still reveled in the community of fur and play that filled the rocky den, and still melted under the caress of her mother's tongue.

But she was different now.

The next few days saw Lop leave the den several times.

She explored the rocks around the den, and found a way to the top of the ledge outcropping, where thick blankets of moss and lichens grew. It was much softer up there, and Lop spent many hours lying on the lush greenery, enjoying the warmth that filtered through the birches. One time she walked around the whole pond, to where the water slowly trickled over an ancient beaver dam, and found a small snake basking on a log. He reacted too slowly.

She ate him.

Years before this pond had been much larger, but a small forest fire had driven Beaver away and his dam had fallen into disrepair. Beaver followed the water's flow for several days and discovered a large marsh, which he engineered to suit his needs.

Hunting was hard now. The puppies were growing rapidly and needed much more food. The small creatures the old dog managed to catch, the frogs, mice, and snakes, were becoming scarce. Her hunting ground was not as bountiful as before, for she had learned well.

One evening, when Dog was returning to the den after a particularly meager hunt, she heard frog sounds from an unfamiliar direction, farther down the woods road, past the birch grove.

The old dog was tired, but it was nowhere near dark yet, so she decided to investigate. For the past week or so she had brought most of what she killed back to the puppies, and had kept for herself barely enough food to maintain her strength. Even so, she extended herself and padded slowly down the trail.

On either side stood large, straight pines. The ground that bordered her path was blanketed with three-foot-high ferns. Here and there amid the giant trees grew younger ones of various heights, which, given a bit of luck and another hundred years, would be giants themselves.

Though the sky was still light, these woods grew darker the farther Dog walked. The road was plainly defined, however, and she continued toward the sound of Frog.

Hare heard her coming.

He was waiting in between two clumps of ferns by the side of the trail, waiting to cross. This time of evening he listened carefully before leaving any protective cover.

Very carefully.

A close shave with Horned Owl earlier in the summer had taught him a valuable lesson.

Listen, look, and listen again before you leap!

Hare heard the dog, then saw her. At first the sounds were like Coyote, but slower.

She looked clumsier than Coyote, so with confidence Hare lurched out onto the trail. He had intended simply to cross over it into the dense cover on the other side.

As soon as she saw the big rodent enter the open, Dog reacted.

She gave chase.

Instead of simply jumping for cover and giving her the slip, Hare turned and bounded down the trail at about three-quarter speed. He was a good judge of a pursuer's abilities. Coyote required ninety percent, Fox about the same, but getting away from Lynx was an all-out effort. A hundred and ten percent!

Dog tried her best to catch Hare, but her aging muscles were simply no match for him. He disappeared handily over a rise in the trail, sought cover to the side, and waited, barely out of breath.

Presently the old dog hove into view. Her tongue hung out the side of her mouth and she walked slowly, stiffly, exhausted by her brief effort. Hare could hear her labored breath as she walked slowly by, totally unaware of his presence.

Dog continued painfully on toward the frog voices. The trail led from the pines through a large spruce forest, downhill through more birches, and finally ended abruptly on the shore of a weedy lake.

Frog voices beeped intermittently.

The old dog sought a soft spot to lie down. Just for a moment. She was well aware her reflexes were not up to par—not enough to catch Frog. Just a little rest first. Just a little.

A sharp, discordant symphony of barks and yips intruded into her subconscious. At first the sounds seemed an addition to a dream of puppies, but they were too persistent.

She opened her eyes.

Night had fallen, but through the darkness there was movement. Only yards away were five adult coyotes pacing back and forth in an agitated way, punctuating their steps with yips and barks. Their lips were curled back and their ears were flattened.

In one heartbeat the old dog went from a dead sleep to sharp-eyed, adrenaline-pumped wakefulness!

One small female split from the group and circled around behind the old, yellow dog. It darted in close enough to nip at her tail, and scampered out of range when Dog turned and snarled. There was no defense here, no tree at her back, no cover of rocks to protect her flankes. Dog was not a fighter. She had never raised her voice in anger in all her fourteen years! She was just a good, old, tired mother dog.

The lake!

She instinctively backed toward the lake, at the same time swinging her head repeatedly as the attackers parried for a nip. They were unwilling to risk injury just yet. Her voice was far lower than theirs, lower and rougher, and it helped keep them at bay as she backed into the water. The coyotes sensed they were losing the prize, and pressed closer. Dog was belly deep now, but the footing was firm, and as one of her foes boldly attacked she grabbed it firmly by the ear. The coyote shrieked. As it lunged over backward it left a trophy of half an ear securely clamped in the jaws of Dog.

By now the adrenaline boost had begun to fade. The old girl knew she was no match for the pack, and instinctively moved farther back into deeper water. The coyotes followed until they ran out of footing, then returned to the shore. Once on firm ground their voices rose again in frustration as they saw their quarry swim away into the darkness.

Dog was exhausted.

Though a true water dog and always a strong swimmer, it was all she could do now to keep her head above the surface. Weakened from hunger and the rigors of this day, she pumped her legs, her muscles fueled only by the memory of younger years.

Far to the rear, coyote complaints filtered across the water, and the old dog swam on into the night. The lake and the sky became one as her energy drained. This was her element, her place.

Her heart knew that.

Her heart knew that, but it was not enough to fuel the flesh of a grand old water dog.

Chapter Three

Lop and her brothers crowded the den entrance, waiting for their mother to return.

It was dark.

It had been dark for several hours, and they had never waited this long to be fed.

Their ears pricked up when distant sounds of the coyote band filtered through the forest, but they paid little attention. The barks and yips of wild cousins were a common sound during darkness hours, and the puppies accepted them as they did the snort of Deer and the moan of the wind.

The five males were restless. Each wanted the best view of the route Dog always used when returning from a hunt. Lop was anxious, too, though her unease was fueled more from the heart than the stomach. Her meal of Snake at the beaver dam earlier in the day tempered the demands of hunger, but she watched, too.

Horned Owl flew silently over the rock ledge and the pups shrank back at the sight of him. They knew nothing of Owl. Instinct alone made them afraid. Large, silent, dark things that move swiftly make any heart pound, and well they might. Puppies this small would be an easy meal for Owl.

Lop nipped and snarled at her brothers, forcing them farther back into the den. They could still see out from there, and seemed content to do so. They had learned not to argue with their sister.

For several hours the puppies fretted and fussed, till finally fatigue overcame hunger. One by one they retreated to the back of the den, huddled together more for emotional comfort than warmth, and slept.

Lop slept alone, by the entrance.

She awoke several times during the night, her senses jostled by the passing of nocturnal travelers both large and small, on land and in air. Once she went to the pile of sleeping brothers, sniffed each one, then returned to her post and slept.

The morning brought a clear sky, a bright sun, and a slight tingle to the air. Six puppies waited on the arrow ledge outside the den. They were *very* hungry.

Lop climbed very carefully down to the ground, much to the distress of her brothers. They whined and moaned, jostling one another about. She looked back at them briefly, then headed through the brush toward frog country.

The pups became more excited as they saw their sister disappear from sight. They even called after her with infant barks, and the pushing for a better view became increasingly rough. Finally one pup fell to the ground. He landed with a *squawk,* a decidedly undoglike sound. When he regained his breath and got to his feet he followed the trail of sister Lop.

The remaining pups, unable to contain their excitement, tumbled from the ledge like a furry waterfall. They quickly caught up with their brother and followed along behind, totally engrossed in this new adventure. They had never been on real ground before. They had never tasted a leaf, nor had they picked up a stick or run. For some moments they forgot the trail of Lop and simply reveled in this newfound freedom, recording new smells and tastes as they ran, stumbled, and wrestled their way through the birch woods.

The first pup off the ledge was also the first to drink from the beaver pond. The others followed suit, filling stomachs till hunger no longer nagged. Full bellies slowed the pace, and the pups soon took a minute or two to rest. Or five, or ten. They could see Lop on the opposite shore, crouching.

She was watching a frog.

He was facing the wrong direction, away from the water. She knew that.

When she leaped, he leaped toward the woods.

Wrong way.

She ate him.

When they saw her jump, the pups came alive. They ran clumsily around the edge of the pond, yipping and yapping in excitement.

The wrong way.

When they came to within twenty yards of where she lay, enjoying her first meal of the day, they found that water blocked their path. The flow over the beaver dam had dredged a pool where it fell, and from there formed a stream too deep and too wide for puppies to cross. One mounted the dam and walked to the spillway where the water flowed. It was narrow, but the sticks were too slippery to walk across. Most of the dam was covered with earth, and had grass and small trees growing upon it—easy to cross. But this center part was a puzzle for puppies. They seemed to know they could never cross. And they did not trust the moving water at all.

Lop finished her frog, got up, and walked toward the dam, the memory of snake meat still fresh in her mind.

She mounted the dam, looked carefully, then walked toward her brothers. They ran and stumbled down its length to greet her.

But they could not get close.

The slippery logs of the spillway threatened.

They could not cross.

Everyone whined and complained, but at least they were together, and after a few moments the sun soothed their nerves and they settled down for a short rest. Lop lay down as well. She did not look at flying insects or waving leaves, as did her brothers.

She looked steadily downstream.

One puppy, the first puppy off the ledge, the first puppy to ease his hunger with a bellyful of water, slowly rose to his feet. He was *very* uncomfortable. In a mysterious way he sniffed about the dam. His brothers watched, wondering. He sniffed the trunk of a young alder tree, then a patch of ferns. A small log sticking up from the dam was next, and apparently it was made to suit, for he slowly lifted his leg. The puppy stumbled a couple of times, for he had never stood on three legs before. Then he peed on that log, and peed, and peed.

The brothers watched wide-eyed.

When he was through, and had all four feet firmly on

the ground again, he looked at each brother in turn. If that puppy could have spoken, he might have said, "Okay, squatters, now that's how its *done*!"

Lop continued looking in the direction of the water's flow. The little stream widened as it wound through the woods beyond the dam, gaining strength from springs that lay hidden along its banks. In the pool directly below the overflow, three tiny fish sparkled as they dashed back and forth, feeding on the larvae of mosquitoes that were swept over the dam. There used to be five. Trout ate two of them. The day before the puppies came, Mink ate Trout.

Lop got up, returned to land down her side of the dam, walked to the little pool, then headed downstream.

The other puppies, anxious not to be left behind, scrambled off and kept pace with their sister. The little stream was but a few feet wide at this point, but no matter how much they fussed and wanted to cross over to Lop, they did not. They were afraid. She was used to water. Had she not successfully stalked Frog? She could have crossed easily. But she did not.

They traveled a hundred yards, passing from birch woods into a forest of pine. The stream widened slowly, but the boy puppies did not notice. They were having too much fun exploring every little nook and cranny for whatever surprise might be there.

Red Squirrel scolded from the safety of a low branch as the group passed beneath. The puppies launched into a flurry of yips and baby growls.

For the moment they were not hungry. They filled their stomachs often from the abundance of the creek, and continued to play, joyful at being free from the confining den.

Four hundred yards into the pines the ground began to change. There was a gentle slope now, and the waters of the creek gained speed. A little farther on a large rock split the flow, forming two streams that continued on and out of sight.

Lop walked slowly along her side, watching the ground carefully. When she came abreast of the large rock, she lost sight of the other puppies. She heard them, but her attention was directed at a hollow log that projected from the land into the streambed.

Upon it rested a large ribbon snake.

The snake had a big bulge just behind its head. He had spent hours inside the log, waiting in ambush for a meal to happen by, and it did. Mouse, thinking the log cavern to be a good hiding place, investigated. He ventured too close to the waiting snake, and became a meal.

Sluggish with the success of his catch, Snake's reflexes were not quite up to par, and Lop was upon him before his primitive brain registered a threat.

She lay down to contemplate her prize. This was the biggest thing she had ever caught! She simply started at one end and worked her way steadily to the other, Mouse and all.

Her hunger completely satisfied, Lop got to her feet and looked across the stream for her brothers. She backtracked up her trail a few yards and listened. She heard distant, happy puppy sounds farther down the hill, so she turned and followed the flow once again.

The two streams spread apart as they ran on toward the distant marsh, and her brothers' voices became less clear with every step she took.

Lop never saw them again.

*   *   *

Through the late morning hours Lop moved steadily on. She was not hungry now, nor did she seem disturbed by her brothers' absence. She was simply becoming acquainted with this new world of hers.

The stream finally reached level land, branched out, and added its waters to those of the marsh. As far as the puppy could see there were dead tree trunks silhouetted against the sky. This used to be woods, but long ago a beaver clan had built a dam, flooding hundreds of acres of fine timber. As the water rose, the trees gradually died, their roots unable to breath under the saturated soil.

Grassy hummocks and stands of cattails had taken hold, and in deeper parts there were rafts of water lilies. In most of the marsh only one to two feet of water covered the bottom, but it was enough to nourish a vast variety of water plants. The plants attracted many thousands of ducks and geese. And Moose was there, and Mink and Deer, Raccoon, Fisher, Heron, and many, many more. Beaver had traded a few hundred trees for an environment that supported many thousands of creatures, but he didn't know that.

When she came to the edge of the marsh, Lop turned north. She continued on at the water's edge, taking her time, noticing each frog that jumped and each bird that flew overhead. The pines were gradually replaced by closely set black spruce trees, so close together that they had no green growth except at the very top, where they formed an almost lightproof canopy.

It was darker in there, and Lop quickened her steps. She did not feel at all comfortable in such a gloomy place. Another two hundred yards and the ground rose slightly.

46

The spruces gave way to pine, letting some sunlight reach the forest floor. Here the ground was covered with a soft blanket of brown needles, and every few feet a touch of feathery green poked through. One- and two-year-old pine seedlings had been set out by the farmer after he cut a few of the giant trees. It pleased him to think that maybe someday they, too, would be giants.

The puppy approached an immense stump, climbed upon it, and sat. It was wide enough to hold at least six puppies her size. From this vantage point she could see far through the woods, down into a hollow that contained what looked like a long, green ribbon. Curious, she dismounted from the stump and headed off to investigate.

Ferns. It was all ferns. They had grown up along a logging trail over the years, and formed a perfect border along its length.

When Lop pushed her face through the dense growth into the trail she looked carefully both ways, then stepped out into the open.

Her heart skipped a beat. A familiar odor reached her, faintly. Ever so faintly.

She thrust her nose to the ground.

Her mother—she smelled her mother!

The slightest trace of her mother's scent remained on the ground, and Lop followed it, head down, nose snuffling to catch every wispy hint of the old yellow dog. Sometimes she went too fast, and lost the trail. Weaving back and forth slowly, she picked it up again, her heart racing at the thought of her mother.

The scent was strongest where the old dog had slept near the lake; her odor still rose from the spot where body heat had driven it deep. Lop smelled coyotes, too, but the unfamiliar smell meant nothing to her. She milled about the site a few moments, then followed a less-distinct trail to the edge of the lake.

It stopped. Lop searched about, foraging back and forth, trying to solve the puzzle, but to no avail. She looked across the lake. The sun was at its height now and sparkled gaily on the wide expanse of water. Lop was cheered by the brightness before her. She was a yellow water dog.

The puppy returned to the task at hand. She had followed her mother's scent to this dead end, and so now, nose to the ground, retraced her steps in the opposite direction.

Back through ferns and pines she went, a little quicker this time, for now she kept her nose to the ground.

Past the place where she found the trail, around two bends, a half mile more, and the mother smell began to fade. She had trouble now, for the scent was so faint.

Birch woods. The logging trail led past white woods. She knew these woods.

Lop stood in the middle of the trail, confused. Her mother had not been at the other end, nor was she here. The puppy sat, and an impromptu whimper eased from her throat as her rump hit the ground. She remained there for some time, puzzled.

Finally she stood and headed into the birch trees. First she came upon the little pond. A tiny frog jumped, making rings on the water, but Lop didn't care. She wasn't yet hungry, and her mind was clouded by thoughts of her mother and the confusing trail. She went directly to the rocky ledge that had meant safety and warmth for so many months, climbed up, and entered the den.

It was not as warm as before. The smells of her brothers

and her mother were there but there were no warm bodies to nestle against now. Lop sniffed around for a while, examining scraps, sticks, and tufts of hair. She found a small mat of yellow hair, picked it up, and went to the front of the den.

The sun was still bright. It was sinking now, but the birches would still shine for a little while.

She lay down, put the tuft of hair between her paws, and watched as white trees slowly turned to yellow, then pink. When lavender touched the papery bark, the tired yellow puppy finally slept.

Chapter Four

Lop awoke before the sun.

She had spent a fitful night, waking several times, only to be reminded of her loneliness and increasing hunger. Restless, she lay at the entrance to the den and stared out into the darkened woods.

As soon as there was the barest amount of light, just enough to see shapes begin to emerge from the night, Lop climbed down from the ledge and walked directly to the woods road. There she reacquainted herself with her mother's trail and began to follow it back toward the lake. It was harder to follow now, but with some effort and casting about she was able to follow the old dog's scent.

It wasn't too long before she came to the spot where her mother had happened upon Hare. Lop hadn't noticed this new scent the day before. It was much stronger than her mother's trail, for the big rabbit had crossed here only minutes before. This was the place he usually crossed, when on his nightly rounds.

And Owl had seen him do it.

Lop was interested in this strong, new smell, and she

followed it easily. It led across the road, went through the fern growth on the other side, up a little hill for a few yards, and ended between two large trees. It ended where Owl caught Hare.

The ground was littered with tufts of fur the big bird had plucked away as he cleared a path to skin and meat. He had eaten well, and had severed one hind leg, which he carried off, a prize for his mate and their two adult-size chicks. Though full-grown and out of the nest, the two young owls were still dependent on their parents for food.

To Lop, what remained of Hare was a banquet indeed. The meat was still warm. She lay down and, with her paws holding the carcass firmly, she gnawed and chewed and pulled, swallowing meat, skin, and even fur. Her sharp little teeth made short work of the softer parts, but they were not yet strong enough to break the larger bones.

Good thing—she might have choked.

Halfway through her meal she was distracted by a creaking noise. She looked up and saw Raven land on a branch high overhead.

Lop held her breath. She knew nothing of threats, of danger. But instinct made her muscles tense. She watched the big, black bird and barely breathed.

He sat for a moment, watching her, then launched from the branch and flew off through the dusky woods.

She breathed again.

When Lop had eaten as much as her little belly could hold, she glanced about, looking for a good place to take a nap. A big meal always made her a little sleepy. Always had.

The woods were beginning to brighten now, and the

cover of ferns along the logging trail seemed a likely place. She retraced her steps, walked back down the short slope, and found a perfect leafy den among the ferns. No sooner had she adjusted her legs in a comfortable way than she fell into a sound and healing sleep.

She dreamed of puppies.

Lop could *hear* them. In the dream they were all back in the den again, waiting for their mother to return with food. They wrestled, yipped, and dashed around the rocky little cave. It all seemed so real. She opened her eyes slowly, saddened to find she was lying in the ferns, and not playing with her brothers after all. Her eyes closed again. Though she wasn't asleep, she still heard puppy sounds. Confused, she opened her eyes again, and just as she did so, Fox walked slowly by, just a few feet from the thicket of ferns.

Lop was very still. She did not move even a whisker, and she did not blink. The fox passed by. A faint skunky smell drifted past Lop's nose. The puppy voices were quiet now.

Just as Lop was about to shift her weight to get a little more comfortable, she saw movement out on the logging road.

Through the stems of fern she saw three fox pups walking along the trail of their mother. They must have been playing when she heard them first, but now they seemed all business. They walked quietly, their ears pricked erect, as though trying to imitate the mother's gait.

When they passed, Lop edged forward through the cover, just enough to get her head out in the open so she could follow their progress.

A few yards past her hiding place the puppies' discipline faltered. They ran, caught up with their mother, and almost bowled her over. They had in mind a wrestling match, not a quiet walk through the woods! The fox's humor allowed a tumble or two, then she spoke to them sharply. They resumed the order of single file and shortly disappeared over a rise in the trail.

The nearness of the little family made Lop's heart pound. She missed her own, desperately, and with no thought for her safety she started trotting up the trail, hoping to catch another glimpse of Fox and her pups. She wanted to see the warmth again, the familiarity, the belonging. She didn't know those things, of course. It was just that there was an ache in her heart, and watching a family such as this made her long for something she did not have.

When Lop trotted over the rise she saw the puppies ahead, walking obediently behind their mother. Near a stump they paused a moment, sniffing it up and down. Probably Squirrel had sat there awhile. They thought it a marvelous smell.

Fox did not stop, and when she realized her pups were not right behind she turned and yipped.

And she saw Lop.

She said something else in a commanding tone, the pups flattened out upon the ground, and Fox walked slowly, stiff legged, toward the yellow puppy. Her ears flattened out to the sides of her head.

Lop lay down. She was not afraid, just curious.

The fox was curious, too. She had never seen anything like this creature before. It looked something like her pups, but it was quite a bit bigger, and had one dangling ear. The color was right, almost. It did not look fierce. Not at all.

Lop rolled slowly onto her side.

When she did that the fox seemed to relax, stood for a moment longer, then backed up a few steps and turned.

Lop moved her head.

Fox quickly faced her again, this time backing several yards before she turned and walked back to her pups. She allowed them up, and the three started along the trail again.

Lop followed.

Several times during the next hour Fox turned around. And each time, Lop stopped. Once, the puppy had caught a hint of her mother's scent, combined with that of foxes, but now they were past the familiar birches, and all she smelled was fox. She wanted to be with them. But all she could do was follow far behind. Once, she came a bit too close, and the old fox bared her teeth. All animals, no matter how unworldly, know about teeth!

Lop kept her distance.

The fox's path led through an orchard and a small field to a paved road. She crossed directly to the other side and turned. When her three puppies reached the center of the road they thought it a wonderful place to play, and started to run its length. Their mother spoke sharply. They tumbled to the side and off into the grass, as though hit by an electric shock. She meant business—they knew that well.

When the four had moved off into the field far enough, Lop crossed the road. She could not see them, but it was easy to follow the path they made through the tall September grass.

The sun was high, the sky was bright, and new smells

surrounded Lop as she walked through timothy, vetch, and clover blooms. A yellow butterfly flew close overhead. With jaunty, erratic wingbeats it flew most gaily, almost as though its purpose was to cheer a lonely dog.

Lop hurried along, now that the foxes were out of sight. The lush second growth was soft, fragrant, and easily bruised by passing feet. Even if the foxes hadn't left a scent of their own, any animal with half a nose could have followed this trail.

On the crest of a slight rise the timothy grass began to thin and give way to shorter growth. Ahead were patches of low-growing blueberries.

Lop stopped abruptly.

She had ventured too close.

The mother fox was facing her directly, with teeth bared! Too close. Too close.

Lop lay down slowly, carefully.

Fox watched her for a moment, then turned and led her puppies farther down the slope, through the blueberries, toward an area of sparse growth. Lop could see clumps of rotting grass there, left over from midsummer mowing.

Fox was walking very slowly. Her head stayed level as she placed each foot carefully upon the ground. Now and then she stopped, the better to see movement ahead. The pups imitated her movements, but they didn't know why. Attention span is not something well developed in puppies of any kind, so when a bit of fluff from a thistle plant floated overhead one of the pups jumped for it. At their age, any excuse for play appealed. Fox turned but did not scold.

Her semistalk into the field was ruined, but she had not come for elusive prey. This was the beginning of cricket month, and today was cricket-lesson day for her puppies. She now led them at a normal pace to the place where grass clumps lay.

The puppies watched carefully as she turned over a wad of the mulchy stuff. Crickets! Small crickets skittered about, frantically looking for shelter. Some jumped, most just lurched with jerky little movements.

Fun!

The pups bounced and chased and leaped into the air, enjoying thoroughly this best game of all. One caught a large cricket in his mouth, threw it into the air, and when it hit the ground he pinned it down with his right front foot.

Then he looked at his mother. He could feel the cricket squirming beneath his foot, but his attention was on his mother.

She caught a cricket in her mouth, crunched it, and swallowed it down. Then she caught another, and another, and another. It dawned on him finally.

These little things were food!

He carefully tilted his paw to see *his* cricket. When he did so, the agile little creature jumped away. The pup leaped after him. Three leaps later, Cricket became fox food.

Good. Crickets are good. A bit on the crisp side, but thoroughly good. The other puppies followed suit, and it wasn't long before their bellies were full of the little black bugs. Together they went to their mother and begged, pushed, and shoved till she finally gave in and allowed them to nurse.

Lop witnessed the whole affair.

She couldn't see what they were eating, but the excitement of the puppies was infectious. She circled slowly around, down the hill, making her own path now. Fox didn't notice. She was occupied with the lesson. Lop was able to sneak up quite close.

Now she could see!

Next to her foot was one of those rotting clumps.

She moved it aside.

Crickets scurried for cover, but she ate three of them before they hid. Lop was more coordinated than the fox pups were, and she already knew that if something wiggled or hopped, it was usually food. She wasn't really hungry, but repeated the lesson several times. Crickets were good, much easier to catch than Frog, but not as good as Hare.

After the pups topped off their lunch of crickets with a dessert of mother's milk, they looked around for something to do. An adventure, of course. But they were full. A nap was adventure enough.

Lop was not sleepy.

She looked around the field carefully, noting especially the large pond at the center. She knew ponds meant frogs. She saw Woodchuck watching her and the foxes, and she saw a big black bird sitting high in a scraggly pine at the other end of the field. There was a huge rock at the edge of the pond, and a thick stand of cattails choked the western shore.

Lop's gaze went back to the area where the puppies slept. Fox was standing, looking directly at her! The two watched each other for thirty seconds or so. Lop wanted to stand, but she didn't dare.

There was no threat in the fox's pose, she just watched. She had never seen a dog before. This creature before her was quite like her puppies. Mostly she did not understand the hanging ear. This was a puzzle indeed; but Fox seemed more at ease, for by now the odd puppy did not seem to be any kind of threat.

She turned, spoke to her own puppies, and started back through the field the way they had come. The pups looked back at Lop several times before entering the tall grass. They were very curious. Usually their mother chased strangers away.

Lop followed the four through the field, across the road, and through the orchard. When they came abreast of the path that led through the birch woods to her old den, the yellow puppy stopped.

She smelled the ground. There was no trace of Dog there, just of foxes and herself. The others had continued on over a rise and out of sight, and when Lop realized she was alone she broke into a fast trot till she could see them again.

Down the log road, through the ferns, and past the spot where Lop had found the remains of Hare, she followed the foxes. The mother knew the strange puppy was following. She turned her head several times during the journey, checking on the newcomer, but she did not stop.

Night was coming on.

Puppies must be safe at home by the time darkness comes. At night, forests are safe for only the fierce and the strong. Puppies did not qualify; neither did Fox. (Mouse thought she did.)

They traveled past the pines, through spruces, up a steep hill to a patch of maples and birches. On the other side of the hill, which was even steeper, lay a jumble of boulders and fallen trees. One giant hemlock tree was all that stood guard over the garden of rocks.

And a garden it was. The rocks themselves were covered with thick mats of lichens and moss. In between them grew clumps of ferns of every size. Some were only inches tall, and some towered over the foxes and Lop, as together they picked their way carefully down the hill.

Together? All of them, including Fox, were concentrating so hard on their footing that they were not paying any attention to who was where. The mother was showing the way, and she heard her pups grunting along behind her, trying to keep up. She was used to that. Lop was most unused to this kind of rough terrain. She followed the third puppy in line closely, so closely that she bumped into him when some damp moss gave way beneath her foot. He paid no attention. He had to concentrate. Had to. He'd tumbled on these rocks before. He didn't like it!

Fox led the group carefully around a particularly large boulder, turned to her left, and stopped. The fox puppies passed her and entered an opening between two other large stones.

By this time Lop was beginning to feel like part of the group, but when she rounded the boulder the mother fox flattened her ears! The puppy's heart skipped a few beats, as Fox made it clear that Lop was not to enter the den. But Lop was not afraid.

Fox followed her pups, then turned around and lay down, blocking the entrance. She watched Lop.

The puppy looked around at the jumble of enormous rocks. It was dark now, and difficult to see very far, but there were many gaps similar to the opening to Fox's den, and she poked her head into some of them. Each seemed like a cave. The mosses were so thick that they

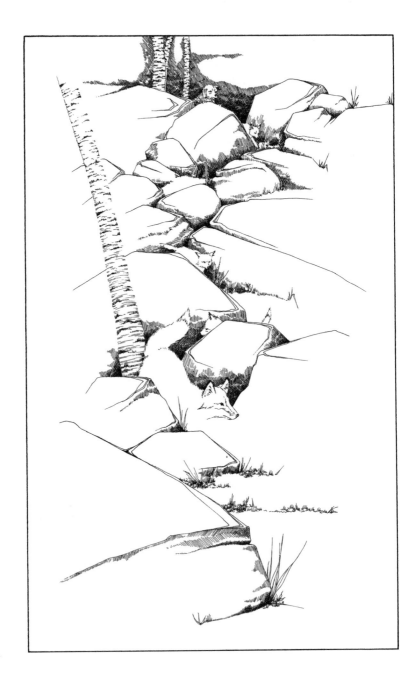

even grew over the spaces between the rocks and made each seem as though it had a roof.

One opening was big enough for her to squeeze into. She did, but found that once inside, she couldn't turn around.

So she backed in. She was close enough to the fox den to hear the muffled grunts that the other pups made as they settled down for the night. It was comforting to be that close, but at the same time it made her lonely. She missed her brothers and her mother. The space Lop occupied had never been a den of any sort. The ground was uneven and damp, and drafts seemed to trickle in from every side. During the night it rained for a while, and water seeped through the moss, down the sides of each rock, soaking every surface inside the little lair. Lop did not sleep well at all. She may have been a water dog, but there was a limit. At least the moss kept rain from falling directly upon her.

A fitful, cold, and clammy night it was.

The rising sun was a welcome sight! The rocky slope faced southeast, and warmed quickly when the sun rose above the treetops below the hill. Lop just lay in her little shelter, letting the sun warm her face. The fox puppies came out and sat on the shallow earth mound in front of their den. They saw Lop's nose protruding from the rocks. They were curious, of course, and wanted to investigate. But they didn't.

Fox finally showed herself.

She stretched her back and neck, yawned mightily, then sat on the mound next to the pups.

Lop wiggled out of *her* little space. She sat, too, enjoying the healing warmth that gradually seeped through her fur.

Fox watched her.

One of the puppies got up and started toward Lop, but a quiet reprimand from Fox squashed the urge.

Enough sitting, enough rest.

Fox got to her feet and walked slowly down and around the big boulder. The pups followed closely. Once the three pups were in single file and moving along. Lop got up and followed suit.

They retraced the difficult route up through the maze of boulders. Fox could easily climb and jump, but the pups were far from nimble and had to take a detour now and then. The second in line, the bold and curious pup, lagged behind a lot, not because he lacked coordination, but because he *was* curious!

Curious about the yellow puppy that followed close behind him.

At one particularly steep place between two logs, he stopped and turned around.

Lop was paying attention to where she placed her feet, and didn't realize the pup had stopped until she almost fell over him! She blinked. They were nose to nose. They sniffed noses. Then Lop gave the pup a tentative lick on the side of his muzzle. That triggered a rapid wag of his little tail, which quickly developed into a total body wiggle. It was a joyful moment, only to be broken by a sharp little bark from ahead and out of sight.

The fox pup quickly turned and proceeded to struggle forth up through the rocks. Lop followed closely, her heart much lighter than before.

Chapter Five

Fox and her furry train retraced their steps of the day before. There were no side trips in the hopes of finding other game, for crickets were the order of the day again. It was cricket month, after all.

Fox looked back several times at her pups and Lop, and though the yellow creature was often on the very heels of the last puppy in line, she did not lay back her ears in warning.

Across the road, through the tall grass, and down the slope they went, to the place where Lop had watched them learn about crickets the day before.

This day she joined the puppies as they turned over clump after clump and feasted on the abundance of little black insects. Every now and then a big one would hop into the air, prompting a playful chase.

Fox watched.

When one of her pups and Lop went after the same cricket her muscles tensed. They both jumped at the same time, collided in midflight, and tumbled to the ground. Fox jumped to her feet.

The pups seemed to forget the cricket, for when they landed a brief wrestling match ensued. Lop was much stronger than the round fox puppy, but she seemed to enjoy giving him the edge. She rolled on the ground as the excited little pup tumbled over her, bounced up, and tumbled again.

The activity stirred up the ground so that crickets were jumping everywhere! One of the other pups scrambled to catch as many as she could, and in her haste fell over the two wrestlers. Then it quickly became a foursome. The puppies rolled and jumped and flung themselves about with absolute glee, totally unaware they were not kin.

And Fox watched.

Finally exhausted, they lay together in the warmth of the sun, oblivious of the fact that three were foxes and one was a dog, and slept.

Fox watched over them.

When the puppies awoke, Fox led them back through the field and down the trail toward home. Lop did not pause at the birch tree trail this time. She brought up the rear all the way to the bouldered slope. Nor did Fox look back. She was aware of all that went on behind her. There were some shenanigans from time to time, but she seemed content that Lop was no kind of threat.

When they reached the den the fox puppies entered as before, and Lop hung back by her little cave.

The sun was high now, the trip back had been strenuous, and Lop's tongue lolled from the side of her mouth.

Too warm.

She backed into her moss-covered cave, where it was cool. She lay just far enough in to feel the cooling drafts, but far enough out so she could see the entrance to Fox's den.

Fox sat for a moment on her entrance mound, carefully surveying the views below. Then she stood and moved off carefully down the hill and out of Lop's sight.

Once Fox had reached the bottom and walked out upon level ground, Lop could see her again, and followed her route off through the trees until she was lost from view.

Lop looked toward the foxes' den. She could see six little pointy ears sticking up behind the entrance mound. She uttered a quiet little "wuf."

No answer.

Lop crawled out into the open, stretched as high as she could, and saw that the fox puppies were watching her.

They were wiggling all over. They wanted to play, and it was all they could do to stay put.

Lop walked up to the den slowly. When she reached the mound of loose dirt she stretched forward, rubbed noses with each puppy, then lay down in a shallow depression that lay between the mound and the entrance to the den. The fox pups let loose then, rolling over her, using her for a mattress, trampoline, and teething toy! The play didn't last long, for they were tired from the journey. Especially Lop. Though she was bigger and stronger than the other puppies, their upbringing had been far more rigorous. Her sinews and joints were not as well developed as theirs, for she was faster growing, and would need more time than they to become closely knit and coordinated.

The female puppy sought the shade of the den. Lop and the two males followed suit. It was not as large as the one in the birches, and it smelled different, kind of musky. There was no room to play in here, but it was snug and cool. Lop sniffed the floor and surfaces of all the rocks that formed the cave. She found the place where foxes slept—the only level spot—and lay down upon it. The three puppies snuggled against her and the four fell asleep. The comforting bodies that pressed against her were a tonic for the orphaned Lop. No more fitful dreams of lost brothers and fear. These warm little hearts were real.

Lop was still sandwiched between the pups when she woke. She felt comfortable, cozy. She heard a slight rustle outside but gave it no further thought. The other three heard it, too. *They* knew what it meant, and immediately jumped to their feet and went outside. Lop followed.

Directly outside the entrance to the den lay the bodies of four fat little voles. The excited fox puppies each took one and began to toss and bat them about. They then settled down and made short work of devouring the little rodents. Lop lay claim to the fourth, and, without ceremony, ate it.

Then she saw Fox down the hill in the distance, heading off to another hunt.

She *thought* it was Fox. But it wasn't the fox she knew as the mother of the pups.

It was the father.

When the puppies were younger, their father was in attendance a good deal of the time, sharing the responsibilities of hunting and baby-sitting, but now the adult male was a less frequent visitor.

This litter was quite late in being born. By September fox puppies usually are developed enough so they may seek dens, or at least shelter, of their own. They often have several, primarily used as safe havens from danger or bad weather, but most of the time they bed down wherever night finds them. It would be a while before *these* pups were ready to wander.

By leaving food outside the den, Fox and her mate slowly taught the pups to be more aware of the world. They got used to the sights and sounds of the woods, caught an insect now and then, and gradually their horizons widened.

Now they knew the trail to cricket country. They knew voles and mice were in that field, and they knew how good those small, furry things tasted.

The puppies knew of feathered prey as well. Fox was particularly clever at catching ducks. Deep in the marsh, where ducks of every description sought shelter and food, Fox played a game that was the downfall of many, especially black ducks.

With a stick in her mouth she would present herself boldly and approach the edge of the marsh. At first the ducks would paddle away and mill about cautiously a safe distance from shore. Then Fox might toss the stick in the air and spend time playing, seeming to delight in some sort of foolish game. She did this to trick the ducks into thinking she wasn't paying any attention to them. But she was.

Before long she moved farther from the water, and crouched, hidden, behind a hummock of reeds and grass. The ducks, their curiosity piqued, would often waddle forth from the water to see where this silly creature they had been watching had gone.

Big mistake.

As often as not, Fox's speed and leaping abilities over-came the ducks' clumsy attempts at escape, and on those days the puppies had a waterfowl feast.

Fox brought them other prey from her trips to the marsh—muskrats, frogs, hares, and now and then a bird; and once she carried home a large chunk of deer meat. She had torn it from a carcass left over from Coyote's hunt. The pups had a tug-of-war over *that* grand prize!

They knew well the odors of different items of prey, and the first time one of the male puppies saw a vole scurry by the den, he smelled only food. That smell was stronger than the impulse to play. He caught it and he ate it. The fox puppies' acquaintance with various types of food was far greater than Lop's, of course, for they had experienced everything their mother's talents allowed her to catch. All three pups were well aware of a basic fact: If it moved, and you could catch it, you could eat it!

The mother fox returned early in the evening, this time carrying three voles and a muskrat in her mouth. The voles were freshly caught, but she had dug the muskrat from one of many caches she used to store surplus food. He didn't smell very good. Lop preferred fresh food.

Fox was well aware that the odd yellow puppy was inside the den. She simply dropped her offering outside the entrance, withdrew a few yards, and lay down. The four tumbled out and began feeding.

Lop smelled different now, more like the fox puppies, for their odor had rubbed into her fur while they played and slept.

Fox was still somewhat puzzled by . . . by what? By a

fourth puppy? She surely couldn't count. Maybe she could. Lop smelled familiar now, she was no kind of threat, she was just *there*. Just there. Fox seemed to accept that fact.

Throughout the month there were more excursions to the cricket field, and as leaves began to color Lop learned of wild grapes and fallen apples. Each time the group passed through the orchard they searched the ground beneath every tree for fallen fruit. At first there were few, but as October wore on, more and more apples littered the ground, and formed a major part of the family's diet. Fox sometimes stood erect on her two hind legs and picked a ripe apple right from the tree.

Raven liked apples, too. Sometimes he was there.

The fox puppies became more and more independent as cool weather approached. They sometimes went on hunts of their own, separately, and slept outside the den, unless the weather was bad. Lop rarely did.

The more aloof the other puppies became, the more she was drawn to the company of Fox. The pups, nearly adults in appearance now that November approached, had extended their territory and expertise far beyond anything Lop had known.

Though her own were rarely home, Fox continued supplying food for the big yellow pup. A *lot* of food. By now Lop was almost twice her size, and still growing, fast.

Sometimes, when Fox was away, Lop went out on a hunt of her own. She was still clumsy, but was expert at catching frogs, and enjoyed hunting in the shallow waters of the nearby marsh. Migrating flocks of ducks and geese rested there now, gaining strength for further flight. Lop watched them for long periods of time, sometimes sitting right out in the open, sometimes lying hidden in shoreland growth or behind a stump.

She had never seen Fox's method of catching ducks, but she knew they were good to eat.

Once, after catching and eating a frog, Lop swam lazily across a narrow waterway to investigate a tiny island. It *was* tiny, perhaps only five yards wide, but it rose high out of the water and had one very large hemlock tree growing at its center. It was a very balanced, odd sight, and seemed out of place in this maze of waterways and dead trees—a landmark.

Nearing the shore, she slowly paddled around a stand of cattails, and the water erupted in her face!

An explosion! An explosion of wings hurled water about Lop's head as Black Duck frantically tried to become airborne.

Lop recoiled, then instinctively lunged at the struggling bird, catching it by a foot. Duck fought to free herself, thrashing the dog about the head, and finally a stiff primary feather caught Lop in the eye. The pain of it made her lose her grip, and the bird launched into the air as if from a catapult!

Squinting with pain, her ears full of water, the dog struggled onto the shore and shook. Water sprayed, and her pointy ear cleared. It took two more vigorous shakes to empty the hanging, water-dog ear.

She did not catch Duck. She did not *eat* Duck. But now she knew how: the same way her mother stalked her first froggy meal—under water.

Lop returned to the den.

Fox was there. She had brought a hare, consumed part

of it, and left the rest for Lop. It was smelly, certainly not as good as Duck would have been.

The old fox was curled up several yards from the den opening. Her tail covered her face when Lop first arrived, but now she watched the puppy eat. It was a puzzle. She never had a puppy hang around this late in the year. They were always off on their own, establishing territories and hunting sites.

Now and again one of her own pups would arrive at the den—just for a visit. But she never stayed.

When she finished eating, Lop climbed up to where Fox lay watching. She moved slowly. She was tired from the swim and the tussle with Duck.

The dog lay down close enough to rest her big yellow head against Fox's soft belly, and slept soundly.

A puzzle for Fox. A puzzle indeed.

Chapter Six

Winter.

No more grapes, apples, or frogs. No ducks. Muskrat was safe in his icebound lodge. His waterways locked from view, he enjoyed safety he could never know during warmer times.

Hunting was hard for the female fox. Now and then she ran across a coyote kill, but she had to beware, and steal a meal when they weren't near. She was no match for Coyote. Many a fox had fallen prey to its larger cousin when snow was too deep for flight.

Her ears were keen. She often heard Vole or Mouse beneath the snow, traveling hidden paths. If no crust barred her way, she could pounce through and trap them with her feet. Sometimes she caught Partridge when he huddled under drifting snow, waiting for the weather to clear. Dried grapes hanging from withered vines were poor substitutes for partridge meat. But sometimes they had to do.

When a crust offered solid footing, Fox often bested Hare in a race across the snow. But so did Coyote and

Great Horned Owl, and the big white rabbits were getting scarce.

Fox struggled hard to feed both herself and the big yellow puppy. Lop caught a vole now and then, but she was not yet coordinated enough to catch other winter prey.

Fox's lush winter coat began to lose its shine, and the layer of fat stored beneath her skin began to thin. All the caches of stored summer kills were long since gone. The two canine cousins, one yellow, one red, shared a den and the winter wind. They shared, too, a lessening of spirit, as daylight and food came in progressively shorter supply.

A twenty-four-hour period passed, during which Fox ventured forth three times, only to return home without food for Lop. Skunked. On a fourth trip she caught one mouse, and ate it herself.

As Fox made her way back to the den, large wet snow-flakes began to fall through the dense canopy of pines and the crusty snow that had covered the ground for several weeks quickly disappeared from sight. Dried ferns drooped low, weighed down by the burden of heavy flakes, and by the time Fox reached the den her rusty red topside was completely covered with a thick blanket of white.

Lop looked out hopefully as the old fox made her way up the hill, but there was nothing in her mouth. Fox approached the den opening, stopped, and shook vigorously, throwing wet snow in all directions. The puppy greeted her with excited licking of Fox's muzzle and both sides of her face, almost as if positive thinking could actually produce some food.

It didn't.

The two animals retreated to the protection of the den and watched as night began to reach through the woods, and they watched as the heavy flakes slowly erased all sign of rocks, stumps, and familiar paths. Screech Owl watched from the safety of her hole in a giant beech tree. Deer watched. Raven watched. They all knew that hard times went hand in hand with the arrival of deep wet snow.

Rodents that were Owl's chief source of food would now spend most of their time in the safety of their snowbound tunnels. Deer would have to depend on immature buds, evergreen tips, and his ability to dig through the snow for acorns and frozen apples. And Raven—he would now rely heavily on the successes of Coyote's hunt, and the remains of those that winter killed. The big black bird was expert at surviving on leftovers abandoned by more powerful hunters than he.

Porcupine? He wasn't bothered by much of anything. Certainly not snow. All he had to do to find a meal was climb a tree, preferably a juicy hemlock tree.

Snow continued falling throughout the night, joining forces with the wind during the wee morning hours. Together they transformed the forest into a world of gentle shapes and thick, white lace. Each low pine bough became a tent, and snow caves formed over every young fir and clump of withered ferns.

As morning light slowly revealed the dramatic new landscape, those furred and feathered creatures who could see from their nighttime perches and dens were silent.

Everyone watched. For some, too young to have lived

through winter before, just the unfamiliar view was sobering, perhaps frightening. Instinct within the more experienced prohibited any compromise with discipline or caution. Those who had done so, did not survive.

Chickadees were the first to welcome the day. They cheerily flitted from tree to tree.

Deee-de! Deee-de! The perky notes seemed to reflect the sun. Crystals of sound is what they were, as crisp and tinkly as light passed through a shard of ice.

The sound seeped through a shallow drift that covered the entrance to Fox's den and woke up the sleeping Lop. She raised her head slowly, and saw that Fox was gone. Light filtered through the snow at the opening, enough so she could see back into the deeper parts of the rocky cave. Fox was not there.

The pup pushed her face through the layer of snow, then her shoulders, then her whole self, creating a tunnel almost four feet long, before her nose reached open air.

The reflections of the sun through the millions of frozen crystals that now covered the ground hurt her eyes, and Lop squinted. She saw a slight depression, a path, leading away from the den—Fox's path. She had left during the night, and by dawn the snowfall had almost erased her trail. Lop had no desire to wade through the deep snow. She did not want to explore or play—she wanted to *eat*. She did a tight turn, knocking down most of the snow tunnel, and reentered the den to wait for Fox. To wait for Fox, and food.

Chapter Seven

"Dad! Hey, Dad!" *Slam!* The bundled-up little boy ran into the kitchen of the old farmhouse, tracking wet snow across the floor.

"Dad! Dad, where *are* you?" His voice rose higher, somewhere between an impatient and a semihysterical pitch.

"Roz! *Roz!*" his father yelled up from the basement. "How many times have I told you not to slam that damn door!"

Roz, Roz, *Roz;* God, how he hated his name! He had been named after his great-grandfather, Rozwell, and how a descendant of a Hessian soldier ever got a name like Rozwell was beyond a ten year old's comprehension. Max, Burt, Luke, *anything* would have been better than *Roz!*

"Hey, Roz! Rozzy, Rozzy, Roz. Howcum ya got a *girl's* name, Rozzy?" There was always some jerk at school who was bigger than he, who delighted in getting away with taunts like that.

"Dad!" The boy took the cellar stairs two at a time. "Dad! One of my chickens is missing!"

His father thought for a moment.

"Well, I'll tell yuh. . . ." He paused again. "Actually I *told* you this might happen. Remember? Those little banties of yours would be a lot safer in the chicken house with the layers."

"But Dad, I can't keep 'em cooped up. They hafta be able to poke around and fly n' stuff. Can't keep 'em in with a bunch of stupid old fat chickens!"

"I know, I know. I like seeing 'em strutting around, too. I know." The man remembered all the beautifully colored bantams he had raised as he grew up on this same farm. No matter how difficult times became over the years there were always a few banty roosters around, carousing, crowing, cheering whoever was within earshot. *He* had never kept them penned up either. He didn't have the heart.

"Well, let's go see."

They climbed the stairs and went through the kitchen.

"Dammit, Roz, we get back in, you clean up all this water!"

The snow was by far the heaviest they'd had this winter. In some places it lay two feet deep, and in others, in the lee of a wall or in back of the house, there were four- and five-foot drifts. There was a ragged path leading to the barn, made by the farmer's legs as he slogged through on his way to morning chores. The boy followed close on his father's heels, trying to step into the foot and leg spaces left in the snow. It was hard going, and by the time they reached the barn the boy was sweat-soaked and out of breath. Old Dad didn't hang back just because there was a little guy bringing up the rear.

The farmer, Dan, had wished through many winters that the ancestor who built this place had seen fit to connect the house with the barns, in the manner of so many New England farms. It would have saved an awful lot of shoveling.

One winter morning after spending several hours shoveling a path out of particularly heavy, wet snow, he sat down and figured out how much it had weighed. The path was two shovel-widths wide, two shovelfuls deep, and about fifty yards long. He weighed one shovelful of snow, figured in about eight complete shovelings per winter (there were more, he counted only the heaviest ones), multiplied that times the number of winters the farm had been there, and came up with the fact that over 3,400 *tons* of snow had been shoveled from that path! He started to figure out how many calories had been burned in the effort, but gave up on that one.

Once inside the barn, Roz and his dad stomped their feet, brushed the clinging snow from their pants, and walked toward the rear, where the lambing pens were. A narrow door led from there, down a step, to what they called the "outer" part. This was a long shed with a dirt floor that hung off the north wall of the barn. It was the entryway into the barn for all the large animals, and provided shelter for them in bad weather. It was partitioned into several areas so that horses wouldn't step on sheep, pigs wouldn't root up the whole thing, and cows wouldn't drop big plops all over the place. The chicken house was attached to the outside wall and could be entered through a small door. The nesting boxes were on the other side of that wall as well, and, by lifting a long, hinged board, you could reach into the nests and collect the eggs.

The banty chickens had the run of the whole barn. They gleaned a living from whatever food they could pilfer from the other animals. Two of the little roosters were even bold enough to drive the barn cats from their dish now and then!

Roz and his father stepped into the outer part and counted chickens. There were five hens together, scratching at a leftover mass of hay in hopes of finding something marvelous underneath. Two more were investigating the pigpen. The two roosters were in the outer doorway, trying to decide whether or not to have a fight. Two more hens were still roosting overhead on a rafter. Eleven . . . one hen was missing.

Roz had long since learned not to name the animals, at least not the ones that got bought and sold, or eaten. All he knew was that one of his birds was missing. Sometimes they just died—disease and winter cold claimed a victim now and then; but these had all been healthy the day before. There were no clues inside the barn.

The boy and his father went through the "rooster" door and looked carefully at the snow out in the barnyard. It had been well trampled by the cows when they had been let out after milking, but there were still large areas untouched.

Dan plowed through a drift that lay against the north wall. Roz went farther out into the barnyard, examining each square foot of ground carefully.

Cat prints. Cow prints. Various little bird prints, chicken prints, sheep prints . . .

Cat prints?

He went back to the cat prints. They were too big. They weren't round enough.

"Dad! Hey, Dad! . . . C'mere!"

His father pushed free of the deep snow and joined Roz, squatting on the ground beside him. He smiled when he saw what his son had found. He knew this little footprint well.

"Remember, Roz? Remember in the summer when we went swimming down in the pond that last time?"

"Sure I do. You just wanted to lie on the big rock and watch the old raven who sits up in that scraggly tree sometimes." The boy knew his father could make up all kinds of excuses to go the rock and watch that old bird. A swim was just one of them.

"No. No, remember when we were looking at the mud and saw what you thought were dog tracks?"

Well, Roz *did* remember that. He thought maybe they had been made by a stray dog, and he got all excited because he had always wanted a dog of his own. He couldn't have one though. His mother was allergic to dog fur. It was funny, somehow. She was real little, but she was strong. She could lug a bale of hay about as easily as any man could. Pretty, too. Prettier than most movie stars. The boys at school used to kid him about that. "Oh boy, Roz—what a mama, oh boy, oh boy!" He kind of knew what they meant, and it made him mad. They were just jealous though.

It just seemed funny that someone that pretty and that strong could be allergic to something.

"You remember those tracks, Roz?"

" 'Course I do. Coyotes made 'em."

"Okay." With the tip of a finger his father made an imprint in the snow that looked like a coyote track, then put the toenail marks in with the tip of a broken pencil he had in his pocket. It was right next to the small track Roz had found.

"Looks just like this one," the boy said. "Well, almost."

His father looked at him for a moment, waiting.

"Fox!" Roz exclaimed. "Fox, fox, fox! A damn fox got my hen!"

Dan put his hand on the boy's shoulder. "Well now, its not a *damn* fox. Its just a fox doin' what comes naturally. Just a regular old, foxy fox."

Chapter Eight

Lop waited patiently for the female fox's return. She went out of the den several times during the morning, totally collapsing the snow tunnel. Now it was partially packed down into sort of a terrace just outside the opening.

The sun was high. It reflected off the snow and warmed the puppy as she lay outside, gazing down the hill in the direction from which she thought Fox would come. Her eyes were half shut, partly because of the intensity of light, and partly because she was drowsy and warm.

Just as she was about to drift off to sleep, Lop heard Blue Jay's shrill warning cry pierce the air. It came from behind her, *up* the hill. Blue jays and little red squirrels were the alarm triggers in these woods, seldom failing to cause a ruckus when something was afoot.

Lop came instantly awake, jumped to her feet, and stretched as tall as she could, trying to see over the snow-covered boulders. She had learned from the fox puppies that when Blue Jay screams, you get ready to hide, for you never know. You never know.

The jay screamed again, much closer this time. Just as the notes tapered off, Lop caught sight of Fox struggling through the deep snow. She carried something in her mouth that flopped and dragged, making it hard for her to keep her head up as she walked. The puppy lost sight of her as she angled down the slope, following the path of least resistance—what remained of her early trail. Lop watched from the new terrace outside the den, and in a moment Fox reappeared, pushing her way through the last barrier of snow onto the small open space. In her mouth she held a partially eaten, medium-sized bird.

Smaller than a duck, it was something Lop had never seen before. When the old fox put the bird down and moved aside, the puppy immediately began feeding. She always had trouble with the feathers on birds. Lop wasn't as clever as the foxes at avoiding feathers and bones, for her mouth and teeth were clumsier than theirs.

She didn't care, she wasn't picky, she ate what was left of this bird, bones and all. All that remained on the ground were some stiff wing-feathers and one foot.

The left one. The left foot of a barred Rock banty hen, a hen that might have won a ribbon at the Union Fair next summer.

That night the temperature dropped. A crust formed on the surface of the snow, permitting all but Deer to walk on top. From inside the den Lop could hear him as he made his way through the woods, breaking through the surface with a *crunch* at every step.

The coyotes heard, too. Four of them followed him cautiously as he wound his way through the spruce woods and out onto the lake. But they waited too long. High winds that drifted snow around the den and throughout the woods had created alleys and huge patches of open spaces out on the ice, giving Deer a chance to run once the pursuers decided he was to be their next meal. Two-thirds of the way across the lake they gave up the chase and slunk back into the deep woods to find easier prey.

Fox left again during the night. She did not keep to her trail of the night before, preferring now to make a more devious series of detours and switchbacks before arriving at the barn. The hard surface made for easy traveling, and she was back at the den before sunrise with one half-eaten and one whole banty hen. For the two animals this was good fortune indeed, and with their hunger satisfied from two hearty meals in a row, Lop and Fox slept soundly most of the day through.

Part of Roz's morning routine was to help with the feeding of animals. The school bus came for him at 7:15, so in order to shower, dress, feed, and have his own breakfast in time to be ready, he had to get out of bed at 5:15. Two hours seemed like plenty of time. He did tend to spend a little too much time in the barn, kind of on purpose. His father fed the cows and horses. Roz fed the cats, the pigs, the sheep, and his own banty chickens. The layers had their own bulk feeder, which had to be filled only once a week. In the warmer weather the boy did the watering as well, but during winter there was too much ice to chop from buckets, and there just wasn't time enough for it all.

He had one other chore. After he came home from school he had to fill the two woodboxes. The house was heated by two wood-burning stoves, one in the kitchen and one in the front parlor. For this job he was paid two dollars a week.

All the other kids he knew got allowances. They didn't have to work for any of it. One big fat girl in the seventh grade got five dollars a week! She spent all hers on candy and potato chips. She was really a nice girl, but some kids teased her a lot, and the more they teased, the more she ate.

Roz fed the pigs first. The buckets were heavy, and he liked to get the heavy work done first. All he had to do for the sheep was put grain in their long trough and fill the hay crib. Cats got a quart measure of dried kibbles.

He dawdled over them some. They always insisted on a little extra attention and *they* were the ones usually responsible if he was running late! At least, that's the excuse he used.

Last came his banty chickens. They were purebred barred Rocks. He was proud of *them* all right. That two dollars a week had mostly gone toward his little flock of prize chickens. Each year they made nests all over the barn—in horse stalls, in the hayloft, under the barn, even outside sometimes. Once he found a nest full of eggs in a hollow log on the edge of the woods. But the skunks got those.

Last spring the hens hatched out almost a hundred chicks. The cats got a few, a sharp-shinned hawk who was hanging around the barnyard caught a bunch, some just didn't make it, and by Labor Day, when the fair was held, there were sixty-eight left. Roz exhibited one rooster and his favorite hen in the 4-H exhibit, and won a blue ribbon for "Best Pair." *Everybody* wanted to buy his chicks. He sold them all in four days for three dollars and fifty cents a piece! Add that up . . . A nice piece of change for a ten year old.

All Roz had to do for his chickens was spread some cracked corn and meal around on the ground. Some were still half-asleep. The smart ones were high up in the rafters and a couple of dumb ones roosted on a low board in the sheep partition.

"Dad! Dad!" The boy's heart pounded as he counted and recounted.

"Dad! There's two more chickens missing!" Roz ran out to the stanchions where his dad was locking in the cows for milking. "I think one of 'em was old Alice, the one I got the prize for last year!"

His father secured the last cow, frowned, and said, "Two things: Either you pen those little dudes up, or find the fox."

"Find the fox?"

"Yes, find the fox. Else you'll lose most of your birds, for sure."

"Well, I'd rather get the fox than coop up the chickens. Don't want to coop up the chickens."

His father kneeled down next to Roz and put his arm around his shoulders.

"I'm sorry, Roz. I'm sorry. I know how much the banties mean to you." Dan knew. He was fond of the perky little birds, too. He also knew that three dead hens could mean over a hundred dollars of lost chick sales at the next fair.

"Tell you what. Tomorrow is Saturday. No school, right? Right?"

"Yeah, I guess so."

"Well, tonight we'll get the rest of your birds caught,

and put 'em in with the layers. We'll have to wait till after dark when they're roosting, but we'll get 'em. Least'ways they'll be safe tonight."

"Okay."

"Tomorrow, you and I will track us a fox."

The trail the old mother fox had made before the snow hardened was about as clear as Route One. It was almost a trench! Dan had kind of hoped it would have been harder to follow, so his son could learn a few things about tracking. A blind man feeling along with a cane could have followed *this* trail.

Over his shoulder he carried a burlap sack half filled with kindling from the stovewood pile, and in his left hand he held an old ten-gauge, single-shot goose gun that had belonged to his father. He remembered what the old man used to say about hunting: "If'n it takes more'n one shot t'git what yer after, y'got no right t'even have a gun a'tall . . . no sir, y'don't." Dan took a lot of pride in the fact that no animal he ever shot at knew what hit it. And that was going some, too, because a lot of what they ate came out of the woods.

Roz carried a smaller sack. In his were some old newspapers, a canteen of water, and four peanut butter and raspberry preserve sandwiches.

They followed the trail through the orchard to the logging road, and when they came to the woods his father took a knife from his pocket, stripped large pieces of bark from a dead birch tree, and put them in his sack.

Roz didn't have to ask why. He knew that if they found a fox den they would try to smoke them out, and nothing makes greater smoke than birch bark.

With almost every step, Dan broke through the crust.

He couldn't have made more noise if he'd been beating a drum! By the time they got into the big pine woods you could even hear an echo.

"Well, Roz, there's no way we're going to sneak up on anything in here, but at least we'll see where this trail ends up. Could be if Fox hears us he'll just hole up, stay put. Sometimes they'll do that."

Roz was light enough so that he didn't break through at all. He could even slide pretty well when they came to a little slope in the snow. Somehow the brightness of the sun and the easy walking masked the ominous purpose of this outing. Even Blue Jay contributed some raucous notes as she followed the two along the logging trail.

Fox heard the jay's distant scolding. She stuck her head out of the entrance, ears alert.

There was something else. . . .

She darted outside.

Something crunched.

It was faint, but it was not the irregular step of Deer. It had a steady beat.

Fox stood on her hind legs, faced uphill, stretched as tall as she could, and listened.

Blue Jay's voice sounded again.

Something unknown was approaching, and for the fox that was cue enough to run.

Run!

She almost did a backward somersault. Actually it was more like the quick turn a cutting horse makes, and when her front feet touched the ground she was already in full flight.

Fox streaked down the hill, half running, half sliding on the slippery crust, and by the time Roz and his father arrived and looked down toward the spruce woods, Fox was out of sight.

Dan knew there was a den here among the boulders. It had been used by different families of foxes long before he was born. He knew of three or four others around the farm as well.

"C'mon down here, Roz." He led the way around snow-covered boulders, following the frozen fox trail cautiously. The boy could step into his father's footprints now. It was steep in some places, and the footprints were very close together. It was hard though for Roz to carry his sack and still keep his balance.

Dan worked his way around the large rock near the entrance to the den.

"Bingo! Hey, hey, hey-y-y-y! We got 'em, Rozzy!"

Roz hurried to catch up to his dad. When he did, he saw the flat areas in front of the opening, and he saw feathers of all sizes scattered about. They were black-and-white, barred feathers.

Barred rock feathers.

"Stinkin' fox," he muttered under his breath.

Dan looked around. He knew the area well, knew it was just a mass of boulders and that there had to be many air spaces among them, good for the draft he'd need to smoke out whatever was in the den. He dropped his sack of wood, put a buckshot shell in his old shotgun, and stuck it, butt first, securely in a drift.

"Okay, Roz. Now let's see. First we'll plug up the entry with a little snow, just enough to keep the smoke in." Roz did that.

"How come we don't pack it tight?"

"Well, we want to keep the smoke in, but if that old

fox is in there we want to make it so she can bust out when she's had enough."

Dan poked around some a few feet downhill from the den, trying to find a likely place to build the fire. He knew there were lots of air spaces that would probably allow the smoke to seek a path uphill and into the den.

"Looks good, looks good. Roz, bring your sack down here. No, never mind, just bring me a handful of the birch bark." Dan dug out a bunch of snow from between two boulders. When he looked up inside, he could see a space that was bare of snow. It led uphill, kind of like a hallway. He took his mitten off, shoved his hand as far into the space as he could, and felt a slight draft.

"Good. We'll try it here." He laid down a small pile of poplar kindling they'd had in the barn for years; he didn't need paper to start it, just touch a match and it went. He did, and it did.

"Pull off some of these spruce tips over there, Roz, they'll make good smoke."

"How come we don't just use the bark we brought?"

"Savin' it for last."

Once the fire was going strongly, Dan put on some heavier pieces of wood. He could see that a good portion of the smoke was being drawn up to the rocky passageway. He looked over the snow and could see spots where it was beginning to turn gray, areas between rocks where the smoke was reaching close to the surface of the snow.

Lop had heard the noise of approaching footsteps when Dan and Roz first neared the entrance of the den. She heard the voices, and never having heard such sounds before, she was puzzled.

Fox was gone. The puppy felt *very* alone. She retreated

90

back into the smallest space she could possibly fit into. When the opening was sealed she squeezed back even farther. She was barely able to see, now that there was but a dim, dim hint of light seeping through the layer of snow.

Lop could hear her heart pounding in her ears. She heard that, and the muffled sounds of voices from outside the den; then it got quieter for a while. The puppy had no knowledge of threats or real danger, knew nothing of humans, and for an innocent of this sort, perhaps bewilderment in the presence of an unknown is the biggest danger. It often translates into a lack of action.

The puppy just cringed there, jammed into the cramped space, wondering what was going on.

Presently an unfamiliar odor reached her nose. It was not an unpleasant one, just not in her experience. It became stronger, and the den began to fill with smoke, making her eyes water. Soon the dim light from the den opening all but disappeared, and something was burning the back of her throat. Greasy smoke from the burning bark began to fill the spaces. She was panting now, and each quick, shallow breath brought a sharper pain to her throat and eyes. What little she could see became indistinct, fuzzy.

Lop became afraid. What little instinct for survival she possessed forced her to inch forward from what could have been a stony coffin. Though almost overcome by the smoke, she dragged herself across the floor of the den to the opening. The effort left her lying on her side, gasping. The last remnants of oxygen were layered near the floor, and what might have been her last breaths sucked it deep into her lungs.

It was just enough. With a desperate lunge, the half-conscious dog thrust her head through the snow barrier into open, clear air.

"Dad! Dad! Don't shoot—it's a dog!" Roz yelled. He had expected a fox to come squirting out of that hole. As a matter of fact, he had already planned to make a really neat hat out of it. People didn't approve of wearing stuff made out of fur anymore, but *this* hat was going to have a little revenge in every stitch!

"Well, I'll be . . ." Dan put his shotgun down and approached the half-conscious dog. "It's big, but I think it's only a pup."

The man reached out, held Lop firmly by the loose skin behind her head, and pulled her gently from the den. The dog opened her eyes, but everything was fuzzy, and nothing made any sense at all. She closed them again.

"I'll tell you, Roz, there's no way *this* critter could ever have caught your hens, no way. She's still too clunky, too puppyish lookin'." Dan held one of her feet. "Anyhow, look at the size of those feet! Durn near twice as big as a fox's!"

Roz hunkered down on the other side of the dog. She *was* big. She must've weighed thirty-five or forty pounds. The boy compared her with different-sized sheep. He was pretty good at guessing sheep weight. He and his dad even had contests doing that.

"A dog. It's a dog, but that's crazy. What's it doing out here anyway?"

His dad didn't have a real good answer for that one.

"Dunno, Roz." Dan paused and rubbed his nose with the back of his mitten which gave him a chance to think for a second. "Dunno. Don't just know. *Have* heard a lot of goofy stories about animals, though. Don't know if half of 'em are true or not." He stood up. It made his knees hurt if he kneeled down too long.

"I'll tell you what it might be—and only God knows how it came about, but I think this here pup was probably raised by that fox, somehow. Somehow. I dunno how, but I'll betcha that was it."

Chapter Nine

Lop recovered her senses in the dark. She felt herself swinging and lurching, and heard the crunch of footsteps through crusty snow. And she heard voices. She didn't know what they were, of course, but there was one that came out in steady, low tones, and another that was higher, a bit piercing at times.

Dan was walking more slowly than he had before. The dog was slung over his shoulder in one of the burlap bags, and it was hard to walk and still avoid bumping her around too much. She was heavier than she looked.

"Dad. Dad. Daddy, pleeeeze. Can't we keep her?"

Roz thought someone *must* have answered his prayers for a dog, if this was the weird way one finally showed up!

"Dad, she can live in the barn. Mom wouldn't have to be near a dog hair, ever!"

"We've been through this a million times, Roz." His father was starting to sound exasperated. The boy knew exasperated was real close to being angry.

"No!"

The rest of the trek home was punctuated only by the crunching of the snow, as the two nursed their own private thoughts of moms, wives, and puppy dogs.

Dan knew darn well that they could have a dog, if it would be an outside dog. Several of his sheepman friends had dogs that actually lived with the sheep. It seemed that they almost *thought* they were sheep. It cut down on the coyote problems, too. But right now he just didn't need any complications. He had enough animals to deal with. Besides, it sure was the wrong time of year to start training a dog.

Roz wanted a dog. He wanted a dog, he wanted a dog . . . so bad! He kept looking up at the big bag slung over Dan's shoulder, and thought that the dog ought to be *his* dog. That wasn't a dog you went to a kennel or a pet shop to buy, wasn't a dog someone brought by because they knew you wanted a dog. That was a dog destiny dropped in your lap in a weird and wonderful way. It seemed to Roz that you owed it to the world's mysterious forces to *keep* that dog, because it was magical.

But Roz didn't say anything more about it.

Lop was carefully rolled out of the bag onto a mass of barley straw in a horse stall. Roz had put a dish of water on the floor and a pile of dried kibbles next to it. They were cat kibbles, but when you don't have a dog, you generally don't have a lot of dog food around!

The puppy had no way of knowing this was not a natural chapter in her life, but she was apprehensive. She was not frightened. She just missed familiar things, and was a little bewildered.

Lop lay on the straw, watching the two creatures that

leaned against the other side of the stall door. They were staring at her, and that made her uneasy. She looked away, put her head down across her legs, and for all intents and purposes, seemed asleep.

But she wasn't.

As soon as Roz and his father left the barn, Lop got up and investigated the bowl. She stuck her tongue in it tentatively, then lapped up half the water. With each swallow the irritation in her throat lessened. She then picked up a couple of the hard kibble bits, chewed them carefully, and swallowed. They were no breast of duck, but they seemed to be some form of food, and she put a goodly dent in the pile.

Lop then sniffed her way around the edges of the stall, not looking for a way out, just sniffing, getting acquainted. Though it had been recently cleaned, she smelled horses, and horse poop, chicken poop, and cat poop; and though she had no way of knowing who all these smells belonged to, she knew poop when she smelled it!

Lop's meal had made her innards begin to react, so in a corner she added her own brand of poop.

Dan had already decided to take the puppy to the pound. Roz knew there was no sense in making a scene. His father had set the rules, and that's just the way it was. It wasn't so bad, the pound was only three miles away and maybe Roz could go see the pup until it got adopted. This place was pretty okay.

Usually you think of a pound as the place where strays get put to sleep after ten days. Not this one. They kept them until they got adopted. There was one old cat in there who was kind of nasty, so no one wanted him. He'd probably been there ten years. Actually, the old lady who ran the place kind of liked him, and when nobody was around she'd let him out and give him the run of the building!

So, that's where Lop went.

She was put in one of two dozen kennel runs that lined the south side of the building. She could not see into the runs on either side of hers, but could see across the aisle into several. One had a small black dog in it who paced back and fourth from one side to the other like a little metronome.

The run to the left of that was filled with a great brown hairy beast who never seemed to move at all. To the right, a large cream-colored mongrel stood with his face pushed against the link-fence gate, looking always toward the door that separated the kennels from the real world.

Lop did not feel threatened by anything that had happened so far. All she knew was that Roz and his father had dragged her from a suffocating, frightening situation, and she had suffered no harm from their attentions. When they had brought her to the kennel she made no attempt to escape. Neither did she resist their touch in any way.

Roz convinced himself quite easily that the reason the puppy was so docile was because he, Roz, *he* had a magic touch and there was already something special about their relationship.

There was. Nothing mystical about it though.

Even in the horse stall, Lop was comforted by the soft sound of the boy's voice. Danger to her had always been accompanied by the harsh cries of Blue Jay, or the quick, furtive movements of Fox, producing emotions with sharp, jagged edges.

But when Roz spoke to her he did it in slow, low tones, as low as a ten year old could muster, and he moved slowly as well. There was no possibility that Lop could interpret anything Roz did as a threat.

The next two days saw Roz at the kennel. After chores on the farm, his father drove him over to visit the lop-eared, yellow puppy. He knew it would be hard on the boy when the pup got adopted, but maybe it would just turn out to be one of those lessons that you need to harden you up. Harden? Well, maybe soften you up. Whatever—a lesson anyway.

Roz sat on the floor in front of the gate to Lop's run. They visited at feeding time, and her dish was placed right up front, so she and the boy were but a few inches apart. Sometimes when Lop tried to push her dish for a better angle at the food, she leaned against the mesh, and Roz could run his fingers along her fur. He spoke to her all the while, and it was a pleasant time for the dog. Comforting. Almost like having another puppy to lean against.

They skipped the third day. Dan had to deliver hay to some people who had horses and didn't have enough space to store a whole winter's supply. On the fourth day of Lop's captivity they went to the pound. Roz had brought an extra large Milk-Bone for her, thinking it would be a nice extra treat.

As they went through the front door the lady that ran the place met Dan's eyes and slowly shook her head.

Lop was gone.

On the way home Roz sat very straight on the seat of the truck. He didn't say anything. He didn't want to cry. There was water in his eyes, but he didn't let it spill over. His heart felt hollow. Dan put his big arm over the boy's shoulders.

"Well, I dunno Roz, you just have to think of it this way"—Dan drew a deep breath—"just think how much luckier that pup is to be livin' in a place where its warm, and where she'll get enough to eat."

Roz didn't say anything. He just turned his head a hair toward the window and let a brimming tear roll slowly down each cheek. He held so tightly to the big Milk-Bone that it broke into pieces inside his pocket.

Chapter Ten

Earlier that day, a heavyset man in overalls had come to the kennel to look for a dog. He had a rough voice, and as he first walked by Lop's run she could smell him. He didn't smell at all like the people who had brought her here. He smelled bad, kind of like the smoke that had made her so sick in the den.

He stopped twice in front of the yellow puppy, then disappeared through the office door. When he returned with the attendant, she had a collar and leash in her hands. She spoke softly to the dog while buckling the collar around Lop's neck.

The woman had explained the circumstances of the dog's capture, that this was not your ordinary puppy and that she would certainly need more than just the normal amount of attention.

"Well, ma'am, looks like she's goin' to be a big'un, an thet's jest what I need." He flashed a toothy grin. Maybe flashed isn't the word, for his teeth, what ones he had left, were all yellowy brown.

"She'll hev good shelter, 'n I'll feed her good. Yuh'cn believe it, sure."

The woman wasn't sure at all.

"We have a policy here of checking up on the animals after a few weeks." She watched his eyes carefully to see how he reacted to her statement. There was none. It was almost as if he hadn't heard her.

Lop hung back a bit, and didn't move when the man gave her leash a tug. His natural instinct was to grab her out by the neck, but he knew that wouldn't sit well with the old lady, so he picked her up in his arms. "Woof . . . heavier'n she looks!"

Boy, did he stink.

Lop was unceremoniously dumped into the back of a pickup with a camper top. There was all kinds of junk inside—engine parts, tires, a couple of broken bags of sand—no place at all to lie down. The tailgate slammed shut.

Lop lost her balance as the truck lurched backward, and again when starting forward. She fell against a paper bag full of bottles, splitting the paper and scattering the bottles around the floor. Every time the truck lurched they rolled against some piece of metal, and finally two of them broke. The puppy managed to find a vacant spot to place her behind, and by bracing herself with her front feet managed to stay upright for the rest of the trip.

Through all this, Lop was again simply bewildered. She had as yet experienced nothing to cause her fear, but some apprehension began to take hold as she endured this rough ride. She was used to soft voices, soft fur, soft touches. This was different.

It was a short trip, probably less than ten minutes. The truck passed through an opening in a tall fence made from old sheet metal roofing sections, drove another hundred yards past piles of old car bodies, and stopped.

The man yanked the tailgate open, and when he saw the loose and broken bottles he yelled.

"You bitch! God *damn* you! Those stinkin' bottles'r worth fifteen cents apiece!" He grabbed her leash and dragged her from the truck.

Lop fell off the tailgate onto her side. She tried to get up, but fell again as the man dragged her along the ground.

"Damn dog. I'll show yuh."

The collar cut off her breath, and she was gagging, gulping for air by the time he stopped and tied the end of her leash to the bumper of an old, rusty car.

"Welcome home, dog." The man's lips parted, revealing the coated brown teeth in what might have been regarded as a grin, down in a sewer somewhere.

He returned to his truck and drove off down one of the alleys between stacked cars, leaving a bewildered yellow puppy standing in the snow. Her throat ached when she swallowed, and her feet were cold. Lop ducked her head and looked beneath the old car. There was a patch of gravelly dirt near the center where no snow had fallen, so she got down on her belly and crawled toward it. The leash was tied too short for her to get totally off the snow, but at least her chest was resting on dry ground.

Shadows gradually lengthened among the piles of derelict automobiles, and when darkness finally came there was an abrupt drop in temperature.

Lop lay shivering throughout the night, unable to

sleep, her muscles trembled so. There was no sign of food or water, so she reached out and ate some snow.

Early next morning, the man returned. After dragging her out from under the car he took the end of a length of chain, doubled it through her collar, and bound it with a piece of thin wire.

"There, that'll hold yuh!" He gave it a yank, just to emphasize the remark.

"C'mon, dog." Another yank. Just to avoid any more hurt to her neck, Lop gave with the pressure of the chain, and walked along behind.

Past two piles of cars, then a left-hand turn, past one more pile, and they arrived at an old wooden packing crate that was on the ground between a tin shack and a dead 1948 Dodge dump truck. The shack had old hubcaps hanging all over it, and inside there were hundreds more, in disorderly stacks.

The man attached the end of the chain to a screw eye on the wall of the shack, and shoved Lop roughly through an opening in the side of the crate.

"There y'are, dog, all the comforts!"

And he left.

Lop could smell that there had been other dogs living in this box before. A large, dirty blanket was crumpled on the floor. It had bits of sand ground into it and all kinds of unidentifiable gunk stuck to it, and there were many kinds of dog hairs clinging to it as well. It smelled terrible, almost as bad as the man. But it was warmer than the ground outside.

There was no kind of logic or wondering going through the puppy's head that day, no thoughts of anger or purpose. Just loneliness, and hunger. And, she did know very well that this was not a good place. Not warm, not friendly, not anything like being with Fox. With Fox she was warm and content. Even in the stall and at the shelter there were soothing sounds and ample food.

This was not a good place.

Late that afternoon the man returned with a metal bowl, put it down in front of the crate, and walked off with an unsteady gait. Lop smelled him, but she didn't come out until he was gone.

The odor from the bowl finally drew her out. She stretched forward to investigate, and found that it held several pieces of bread, some scraps of lunch meat, half a pickle, three moldly saltine crackers, and about three ounces of chocolate milk. Lop knew none of these things. But they smelled edible, and she ate all except the pickle.

That night she slept.

After Lop had been two or three weeks at the junkyard the chain was taken off and she spent an afternoon in the office. That day, the woman from the animal shelter came to see where the puppy lived. The smelly man *knew* she was coming. When she left, Lop was taken back and chained to the metal shack once again.

The man staggered some on the way, for after the woman had left he opened a bottle of dark liquid and consumed more than just a few swigs. When he rewired the chain he fumbled more, leaving it looser than it was before.

The next three months were uneventful for Lop. She concentrated on sleeping, staying warm, and eating whatever odd things were put in her dish.

As the winter wore on, Lop learned not to expect anything to happen on schedule. Anything? There was really nothing other than food to expect, and that came irregularly, sometimes not at all. She learned that when the man swayed and stumbled, those were the days she might not get fed. Or at best, what was offered was leftover people food. Her regular diet of dried kibbles was usually offered by the cup, but sometimes enough for a week was left in and around her bowl. During those times the man was absent for days, and her bucket of water often went dry. In spite of the conditions, Lop did grow. She grew into those big feet, and by the time the last remnants of snow had melted from the yard, she weighed close to eighty pounds. Several times, during days when he did not stagger, the smelly man loosened her collar a notch, for her neck was getting thick. She did not like it when he got that close.

And so it went.

Lop saw other people in the junkyard from time to time, although they rarely came back as far as her box. Sometimes one would visit and rub her hanging ear. When they would turn to go she followed them till the end of her chain caught her up. Sometimes if she bounced on her front legs and whined a bit, they would come back for a few minutes more.

Warmer weather brought more people, and it brought birds as well. During winter Lop saw none close by, but now sparrows came to steal from her dish, and starlings sought out nooks and crannies in the piles of dead cars, for nests. At least now she had more things to watch.

She listened, too.

Late one night, somewhere near—not too far—a hopeful peeper frog called for a mate.

Lop's eyes opened wide! Her heart skipped some beats as she waited for the sound to repeat.

It did . . . and it did . . . and it did.

She remembered birch trees and puppies and a rocky den. And frogs.

And how good frogs tasted!

Again, late one night, after falling to sleep accompanied by the voices of frogs and visions of pine trees, orchards, and fields full of clover and crickets, Lop was awakened by a metallic sound, a sharp *clank*.

She edged forward so she could see out the opening of her box, and there, by the far corner of the metal shack was a dark figure. Then there were two. Each carried a large sack.

Lop remembered sacks.

They made hardly any sound and said nothing as they picked hubcaps off the nails that held them to the walls. Then one took out a long bar and pried the hasp from the ill-fitted door. Both men went inside, and when they appeared again it was obvious that both sacks were very full.

Lop had no experience with visitors during the night, she just hoped that maybe they would come over and give her a rub, or a treat of some kind. But they didn't. They left as quietly as they had come.

Early the next morning Lop heard the unsteady footsteps of her captor approach. That sound usually meant food. She stood, stretched, and ambled out of the crate, wondering what odd thing would be in her bowl this time. She was met by flying food! The bowl narrowly missed her head and the food it had held splashed on her and the ground around.

Loud curses rang in the air as the smelly man staggered around the tin shed.

"Goddamn sneaky bastards! They done it again!" He banged his fists against the jimmied door, partly in frustration, partly to help keep his balance.

"Stinkin', sneaky little snots!" He looked over at the dog. "You! Yer' supposed't *bark*, damn ya!"

With that, he picked up an overlooked hubcap and came at Lop swinging. The first blow caught her alongside her head. The shock of being attacked was worse than the hurt. Lop was a gentle water dog. She didn't know anything of meanness at all. But she knew enough to back up when he staggered toward her again!

He missed the next attempt, lost his balance, and fell to his knees.

"Goddamn dog, I'll learn ya!" He grabbed the chain, worked his way closer, and began hitting her across both sides of her face with all his might.

Lop finally knew what mortal fear meant. Self-preservation overcame her gentle nature and she lunged backward time after time, trying to avoid the blows. His breath and clothes smelled heavily of smoke and old sweat and even that added to the rush of adrenaline, and made her struggles far stronger than he could have expected.

Her collar slipped over one ear. With the next vicious yank it cleared the other and slipped from her head, sending both man and dog falling backward.

"Ooof!" The man's wind was knocked from him. He

108

rolled on his side, clutching his fat belly, and gasped for breath.

Lop picked herself up, looked at him for an instant, turned, and ran. She ran as hard as she could down the alley, farther back into the junkyard. It all looked the same, just one pile of stacked cars after another.

The man regained his feet, and she could hear him cursing behind her, getting closer.

She looked from side to side. Nothing. More alleys and more cars. Straight ahead stood a fence made from other junk—boards, sheets of old metal roofing, broken plywood. She ran toward it, then turned left.

Lop had to go only a few feet before coming to a large gap at the bottom of the fence, and she slithered through it. On the other side stood a seedy patch of woods, and beyond, a slow-moving river.

She ran through the woods, dodging stumps and fallen trees, and upon reaching the other side she rested for a moment. Lop's sides heaved from all this exercise. She wasn't used to it.

When she'd calmed down a bit, Lop approached the water's edge.

A little frog jumped!

She took a long drink, looked up the river and down, then walked into the water. When it was nearly to her shoulder she struck out boldly into the current. Far to the rear Lop could hear the man banging on the junkyard fence, cursing to the sky: "Stinkin' ungrateful dog!"

Chapter Eleven

Lop swam strongly. She was energized by her new freedom and the familiar sight of cattails and water birds along the shore. Partially webbed feet inherited from her grandmother propelled her through the slow-moving river with a power lacking in any but a true water dog.

The river was not very wide, perhaps a hundred yards. Lop swam with the current, its flow aiding in putting distance between her and the junkyard man.

When she could no longer hear his voice, she angled in toward the opposite shore and landed in a large stand of cattails.

There were no buildings on this side of the river, no piles of old junk cars, just cattails. Beyond them was a plain of thick marsh grass that reached to a shallow bank where alders grew, and willows. Then on higher land, a stand of oaks with some of last fall's brown leaves still clinging to the limbs formed a forest. Here and there a feathery green hemlock tree struggled up through the hardwoods, trying to establish a dynasty of its own.

Far in the distance, down the river, Lop could see dark

patches of familiar pines standing out against bare limbs of hardwood's early spring.

She picked her way along the river's edge, heading for the pines, and looking for Frog.

Throughout the day Lop kept up a steady pace. The sun was high, the day quite warm, and she found numerous frogs in the shade of overhanging vegetation near the water.

Only one road crossed the river. A wire mesh fence that went as far as she could see blocked her way across the pavement, and without hesitation she trotted down the bank to the water and swam underneath the bridge, almost as if she had made that journey before. She hadn't, of course, but there seemed to be a purpose to her course. Not just wandering, not just trying to get away from an unpleasant place, she was headed somewhere.

By nightfall the bordering oaks had thinned out, replaced by more hemlock trees and more than just a few huge pines. Lop turned away from the river and pushed her way through thick, dry marsh grass until she happened upon a beaver trail.

The grass was trampled down, forming a miniature roadway through high walls of last year's growth. She followed it toward higher ground and found where the beavers had been harvesting willow shoots. She could smell them. She'd never smelled beaver before.

From this miniature logging yard she trotted a few yards uphill and came across a well-defined trail that paralleled the river.

Deer! She remembered that smell. Something about the familiarity of the odor put her more at ease. She followed the trail at a more relaxed pace than she had used during the day, every now and then stopping, raising her nose to the air, checking for anything else familiar that might drift her way on the breeze.

It was almost dark now.

As she progressed, more and more small, closely spaced fir trees grew alongside the trail, and the ground beneath them was thick with shed needles—an inviting sight for a very tired puppy dog.

Lop searched the uphill side of the trail carefully, looking for a likely opening in the foliage. When she found one, she scooched down on her stomach, crawled back underneath the low-hanging limbs, and only five feet off the trail found a shallow depression in the ground. There was a huge, rotting pine stump sheltering one side, and thick firs roofed it over.

Lop looked back over her shoulder at the trail, hardly visible through the thick boughs, circled several times, and lay down on the first bed of her own choice in many months.

Sleep came quickly.

A thick gray mist hung over the river the following morning. Unlike fog, it slowly swirled and moved like thin smoke as the sun began to warm the air.

Lop had slept soundly, confident in the ability of her one erect ear to warn of any danger. Once during the night she had awakened briefly when a faint, high-pitched "Ma-a-a-a" drifted through the woods. It sounded vaguely familiar, but she gave it no thought.

Now she lay facing the trail. With her head resting on the ground between her paws she could just see out from under the fir boughs, down through the woods, all the way to the marsh-grass flats and the river. Her previous day's swim and the night on a bed of fragrant needles had all but erased the remnants of junkyard smell from her fur, and Lop simply rested for a while, enjoying the feeling of cleanliness and freedom.

She saw a wood duck launch itself from a hole in an old beech tree. She remembered ducks.

She snoozed a bit, only to be shocked awake by the alarmed snort of a deer who had been walking slowly along the trail, pausing occasionally to pick acorns off the ground, acorns Squirrel had missed.

Lop's scent was something new for Deer. It did not instill fear, only caution. She continued walking, but with stiff, short steps, nose raised, searching for an answer to this new riddle. She passed by the motionless puppy, unaware that Lop lay only five feet off the trail. A slight breeze erased the cause for her concern, and she relaxed and concentrated again on her search for treats.

Once the deer was out of sight, Lop crawled out onto the trail and stretched. Her muscles were sore from the exertions of the previous day, and one eye was partially swollen shut from the hubcap blows, but she could still see out of it.

This would be a slower day. The compelling urge to travel she had had the day before was no longer in her. She was not particularly hungry, nothing urgent seemed at hand, so she simply ambled along the deer trail, stopping now and then to sniff at emerging fiddlehead ferns, old stumps, dried deer droppings, and whatever else piqued her interest.

Then she heard the creaking.

Lop looked up. Raven! Raven flew directly over head, close enough that she could see his eyes. He flew over the oaks, uphill through the pines, and a few seconds after he was lost from sight Lop heard him utter his guttural "Croak!"

She remembered Raven, too.

And she followed him.

Slowly. For the ground was uneven, steep, and littered with large rocks and fallen trees. The ground beneath the oaks was littered with dried leaves and small branches. Not even Deer could walk quietly here. Farther on, where pines mixed in, there was more moss on the rocks, and ferns, and many downed trunks were big enough for walking upon. And Lop did.

After an hour of carefully picking her way, she paused by a hollow, mossy log of great size whose side had partially rotted away. Curious, she stuck her head in.

A white-footed mouse practically jumped in her mouth! Lop flicked her head, gathered it up, and swallowed it whole. Pleased with that piece of luck, she lay down alongside the log and washed both of her front feet.

That would have been enough action for an average morning's walk, but as she rose to continue on her way, Lop saw movement ahead. About forty yards distant, crouched low on a log, an *enormous* black cat perched, frozen.

Lop lowered herself slowly, just holding her head high enough to keep most of the cat in sight. It was an awkward position, and her muscles trembled with the effort.

The cat moved one front foot forward ever so slowly. His head did not move at all. Then a hind leg was placed carefully, farther down the side of the log. The other front leg slid slowly ahead, and the whole body then eased forward like a great, furry snake . . . and stopped. The huge yellow eyes seemed not to blink at all.

114

Lop flinched as the cat became a blur. It leaped, and met a whirring partridge three feet in the air! The drum-roll sound of the frantic bird's flight was cut short before they hit the ground.

Lop stretched up to see. She couldn't.

But Cat knew she was there. He did not eat his prey, as he otherwise might have done, but gathered it up in his mouth, leaped back upon the log, and turned toward the guileless puppy.

Lop blinked. Cat bore into her with an unwavering, owl-like stare, then lowered his lids slowly, turned, walked the length of the log, and dropped from sight. His manner was that of one who owned this piece of woods, which, of course, he did.

Lop did not move for a moment, When she was sure that Cat was gone, she picked her way carefully forward. Five feet from the end of his log, nestled between the roots of a long-dead tree, was a small nest. It was lined with light, barred feathers from the chest of Grouse, and contained eleven light tan eggs, still warm.

Lop tried to pick up one of the eggs, but it and two of its neighbors broke. She lapped up the slippery liquid, relishing the feel as it slid down her throat. Without hesitation she broke the rest and gobbled them up, shells and all.

Then she set out to follow Raven's route uphill.

Four hundred yards more and the woods became a forest of old pine. Seedlings and young trees replaced the rocks and fallen trunks she had passed earlier. Here and there small firs struggled for light, but they hadn't much hope of growing large in the shadows of the giant pines.

Lop walked through the forest easily and in silence, for the ground was covered with a thick layer of needles. A large stonerow crossed her path at the top of the hill, and beyond it lay open land. The stonerow was four to five feet high and fifteen feet across, the last resting place for rocks cleared from the field over a two-hundred-year span of time.

The puppy climbed the sloping pile of stones, stood at the top, and stared out into the field.

And Raven croaked.

Lop's heart jumped a beat!

She looked to her right, toward the end of the field, and there, at the very top of a scraggly old pine, sat Raven.

Lop jumped from the row of stones, ran into the field, over a slight rise, and there stretched out below her was a pond. *The* pond! The pond in Fox's cricket field!

The excited puppy ran downhill and crashed into the water where the cattails grew! Dried seed-heads exploded into puffs of fluff when she hit the brittle stalks, and a dozen frogs leaped for their lives. Old Heron almost fell over backward in surprise. She blurted two squawky croaks of her own as she beat the air, trying to remove herself to a neighborhood less unruly.

Lop swam directly across the pond, made a small circle just to celebrate a bit, then climbed out upon the bank and lay down. Mouth open, tongue hanging out to one side, she gazed across the field and back again. If one could ever say that a dog could smile, then surely this yellow water dog was doing just that!

She lay there over an hour.

She watched Woodchuck watching her, and saw a pair of broad-winged hawks soar across the field and enter the pines. She saw that the grass was different, all matted down now, from the weight of winter snow. But one lone thistle still stood tall, one thorny, arrogant thistle with a promise of more to come, for Goldfinch.

Lop finally rose and walked slowly up the hill, across the field to the road, through the orchard, and down the logging trail she knew so well, and when she reached the birch woods she turned toward her birthing den.

Lop stood at the base of the rock outcropping, looking up the ledge, and it didn't seem high now at all! She jumped up upon it, walked to the opening of the den, and cautiously stuck her head in.

Others had been there during the winter months. She smelled raccoon, squirrel, and some fox as well.

It was empty now.

Lop squeezed through the entrance, turned around, and lay down facing the brilliant white woods and the pond of her first frog. The sun was heading down and would soon turn the woods to pink and gold, but the puppy did not wait. Feeling contented and safe, she rested her head on her paws and slept.

Chapter Twelve

For the next several weeks Lop revisited the hunting grounds of her puppy days. The pond in the birch woods held a steady supply of frog treats, but a young beaver was now in residence, and often objected to her presence, demonstrating his displeasure with well-timed smacks of his tail on the surface of the water. If she came too close to his house, he would swim circles around her, punctuating them with loud slaps and surging pirouettes that made the water around him boil, and created a deep sucking sound. She was not afraid of him, but his antics made stalking for frogs impossible.

Lop followed the stream all the way to the marsh, several times. And as many times she caught herself a duck, by hunting submarine-style. She missed more than she caught, but in time the technique provided many a meal, most of which she ate on the tiny island that bore but one giant tree.

One afternoon she was on the island enjoying a meal of duck when she heard a sound. Looking up and across the water, she saw two coyotes staring directly at her! Only fifteen yards of water separated them from the island, but they were not good swimmers, and only a desperate chase for deer ever coaxed them off dry land.

Lop stood. She lowered her head, and for the first time in her life a low rumble began in her throat. It grew in volume slowly and then she opened her mouth and bared her teeth. The sound that issued forth was more venomous and rasping than any growl these coyotes had ever heard! They lowered their heads, dipped their tails, and disappeared quietly back through the alders and into the darkness of the thick spruce woods.

Lop lay down and finished her meal. She also stayed on the island that night. She was twice the weight of a coyote now, but certainly not a practiced fighter, and she still had a puppyish mind. The island seemed a prudent place to sleep.

For the next several weeks she alternated sleeping sites between the den and the island. Lop detoured and visited the rocky den where she had been captured, but found that it still smelled of smoke. The odor, and the fact that now her bearish head would barely fit through the entrance, dismissed it forever as a possible shelter.

Blackfly season came and went, causing little discomfort, for Lop was heavily furred. The only targets available to them were the dog's eyelids and nose, and she quickly learned to tuck her face under her tail. She also found that on bad bug nights the den was far preferable to sleeping in the open.

On her hunting forays Lop became very aware of the

presence of coyotes. Sometimes she saw them trotting through the woods in their fluid, peculiar way, and once she came upon a lone animal scavenging on a carcass that others had killed the day before.

He was intent on getting a bellyful and did not hear her coming up behind; and when she was but four yards to his rear Lop issued forth her now perfected snarling growl.

Coyote nearly turned inside out with fright! He leaped into the air, and hit the ground running. At about fifty yards' distance he turned and stared at the big yellow dog. Just for a moment. He then gathered his dignity and walked slowly away till he was out of her sight.

Lop then feasted on relatively fresh venison, as much as she could possibly eat.

Sometimes she saw coyotes, two or three at a time. Then, instinct came to her defense, and dictated a dose of caution. On those occasions Lop hugged the ground and watched quietly. She had found during her learning days that silence was her greatest ally, and she had also found that movement was a giveaway. It was often just the slightest move that gave Frog's hiding place away, and made a meal of him. Though Lop was not a color one would think of as camouflage, if she did not move, her yellow coat could be easily confused with a patch of sunlight lying on the forest floor.

Once, when she was trotting down the woods road between the rows of ferns, she passed a coyote and was unaware. He was hiding where she had been when she first saw the family of Fox.

He was one of those who had watched her on the

island, eating her first meal of duck. He remembered well the threat of her growl, and as she passed by, *he* was prudent enough to hold his breath!

Throughout early June the days were warm and the blackflies less evident, and Lop spent more time deep in the marsh. After three consecutive days hunting and sleeping on the little island she returned to the den in the birches.

Something was different—many of the trees had been cut.

As she lay in the den looking out on the scene she saw some standing, some lying on the ground. Perhaps if she could have reasoned there would have been some question of confusion, but there wasn't. It just looked a lot different than before.

The trees had sprouted from seed soon after a small forest fire, and had taken root too close together for normal, healthy growth. Dan had cut a third of them down in a very selective way, giving the rest more light, more room to grow.

Normally, small birch has little commercial value, and the trees are left to rot. It is not a waste, for the rotten wood provides precious nutrients for the soil. But Roz saw a chance to add a few dollars to the money his flock brought in.

"Hey, Dad?"

"What hey?" his father answered. "Hey, what?"

Roz's mind was always working.

"Could I have all those trees you cut down yesterday?"

Dan smiled, and kind of chuckled at the same time.

"Well, sure, Roz, but what on earth would you want *them* for?"

"I was thinkin', I was just thinkin'. I know they aren't much good for firewood, but you remember that old guy from the city last year who asked if he could have some birch sticks to keep in his fireplace all summer so it would look pretty?"

"Sure I do." Dan already guessed what Roz was up to. "Sure do."

"Why wouldn't it be a good idea if I cut up some of those trees and tried to sell 'em?"

"It would be. Would be." The man knew Roz had been dying to try using the chain saw for the last year or so. "But you'll have to cut 'em with the handsaw."

The boy's expression hinted at disappointment, but the idea of making money was uppermost in his mind.

Roz thought for a moment.

"I'll bet old Mr. Farley would let me put some down in that new garden section he's got at the feed store—d'you think?"

"Yup, bet he would, bet he would." Dan stood up. "C'mon, Roz, 'bout time we go feed, and we'll see if we can find you a saw."

Roz was up before light. Summertime, boy, he loved summertime! No school. After chores most of the day was his to do as he pleased. Sometimes one or two of his friends would be brought over for the day or even overnight, and they'd have all kinds of adventures.

Making forts out of bales in the hayloft was one of Roz's favorites, or swimming over in the pond. Once they built a little lean-to up on the big rock out in the birch woods. Actually, *he'd* built it—they didn't know much about woods stuff.

When he walked through the orchard Roz stopped at a new dwarf tree he and his dad had planted early in the spring. They had sent away for it. It had limbs grafted on from five different kinds of apple trees! He could see where the grafts were. Boy, five different apples. He thought, If you can do five, why couldn't you have one with *fifty* kinds?

You could.

He thought that would be a good thing to try.

When Roz reached the birches, he thought the best thing to do would be to count the number of cut trees that were small enough in diameter for his purpose. He had figured that anything more than three inches thick would take too long to saw through to be practical, moneywise. He didn't yet know what "labor intensive" meant, but he well knew the consequences of the term: less profit.

He set down the little knapsack he had brought along. It had a canteen of water in it, two peanut butter sandwiches (one with raspberry jam), and a handful of saltine crackers. There were two Band-Aids in there, too. His mom had put those in, and a pad and pencil. The saw was a folding limb saw hanging over his shoulder on a piece of baling twine. He kept that.

Count. Then figure how many eighteen-inch pieces each tree could be cut into.

Count. Within half an hour he had found twenty-seven trees just the right size, between two and three inches thick. There were about twenty feet that were usable in each trunk before it got too limby, near the tops.

He went back to his knapsack and got the pad and pencil. It took some figuring of a kind he hadn't had much of in school yet, but he came up with a total of 351 pieces. Wow! The only thing was, he didn't have a clue how much he could get for them. But it sounded good.

Roz took the saw from his shoulder, unfolded it, and attacked the first tree.

At the first sound of the saw teeth biting into wood, Lop woke up, alert. She pulled herself to the front of the den and cautiously looked out into the birches. The sawing stopped.

At first she saw nothing. Then Roz began sawing again, and she saw some movement through the trees. At first the dog didn't recognize a human form—it was too fragmented by the many trunks that stood between her and the boy. But when Roz stood up and moved ahead to his next cut, she recognized him for what he was: the first person she'd seen since escaping from the junkyard man. The dog edged a little farther back into the den, and lay down to watch.

Roz carried on, and cut the whole first trunk into pieces. It was more work than he thought it would be, but he didn't rest until a whole one was done.

Then the idea of peanut butter and raspberry jam drifted through his mind. Too early for lunch. Probably wasn't yet 8:00 A.M.! But a snack wouldn't hurt. He walked back, picked up the knapsack, went over to a mossy rock near the pond, and sat.

The cool moss felt good on his behind, and as he nibbled on the corner of a sandwich, he reflected upon the niceties of a moist mossy seat, and the fact that he probably wouldn't see the new beaver at all. About the only time Roz and his father had ever seen him was in the evening, when he came out to collect willow shoots. One of the trees Roz had counted was near the shore, but it wasn't one his father had cut. Beaver had done it! He had probably intended it for his dam, but it had fallen the wrong way.

A red squirrel chattered over by the giant rock. Roz liked squirrels. Once, when he was sitting quietly on the stone wall by the road, a squirrel that was using the wall for a trail hopped right across his lap. Roz knew about holding still.

He looked toward the sound.

What he saw then made his heart almost stop! No little red squirrel. What he saw was a domed patch of yellow fur with a pointy, upright ear attached!

Roz held his breath. He could feel the blood pounding in his ears as he slowly moved to stand. He raised himself off the moss a quarter of an inch at a time, till he was standing as tall as he could. If he could have stretched his neck four feet long, he would have gladly done so.

There, underneath the ear and dome of fur, lay two dark, unblinking, liquid eyes.

The boy's mouth sagged partway open, as though waiting for words to spill.

The dog, he thought. The dog, the dog, the dog we caught in the den last winter! Roz closed his mouth, for fear a sound might come out and shatter the dream. But it wasn't a dream—it was truly the lop-eared puppy he saw!

Lop, ill-at-ease under such scrutiny, edged slowly backward into the den.

In spite of the many people she had come in contact with at the junkyard, there were only two humans that stuck in her mind. One was the owner of the yard, with the attendant memories of cold, the inconsistent and oddly varied supply of food, and, of course, the beating she received at his hands.

The second was this boy.

She remembered well the gentle voice and quiet manner he had about him. Unthreatening.

Roz had long since learned the value of quiet and patience when dealing with not only the farm animals, but with an occasional wild one as well. The squirrel on the stone wall was a perfect example. Like all of them, Lop was quick to trust when confronted with a gentle and patient heart.

The sawing noise did not resume.

Lop remained farther back in the safety of the den for a long difficult time. She wanted to move forward and see. For perhaps half an hour she hung back, but finally she couldn't resist, and edged up to the opening.

The boy was gone.

At least there was no movement in the area where he had been.

Lop edged out farther, so her head and shoulders were in the open air. She saw nothing but trees, but did smell something peculiar, something rather good. On the ledge just to her right, only two feet from her head, lay half a peanut butter sandwich!

She studied it a moment, then pulled her front end close enough to give it a careful sniff. It had a lovely smell. She picked it up, pressed it against her palate with her tongue, then chewed twice and swallowed.

Lop lay full length upon the ledge now. She carefully ran her nose back and forth over the spot where the sandwich had lain, not in hopes of finding more, just enjoying the aftersmell.

The sun was high enough to have warmed the ledge, and now was repeating the gift for the dog. She was tempted to nap, but the lingering sandwich smell became mixed with another—raspberry jam—and human, too. Lop looked around the woods, along both sides of the ledge, then overhead, up through the masses of ferns that grew from niches and cracks on the face of the rock.

Another sandwich was growing there!

It hung close to the lichened granite, shaded by a cluster of rock-cap ferns.

And there were five fingers attached.

"Hello, dog."

In an almost inaudible whisper, Roz sent other words down through the ferns to the big yellow dog. She could see only the hand and the sandwich; the rest of him was lying on top of the rock, and had been for quite some time.

Roz knew how to get through the woods making little or no sound, stepping on stones, masses of moss, and now and then a fallen trunk. After first seeing the dog he had quickly traversed the leaf-covered ground by bal-

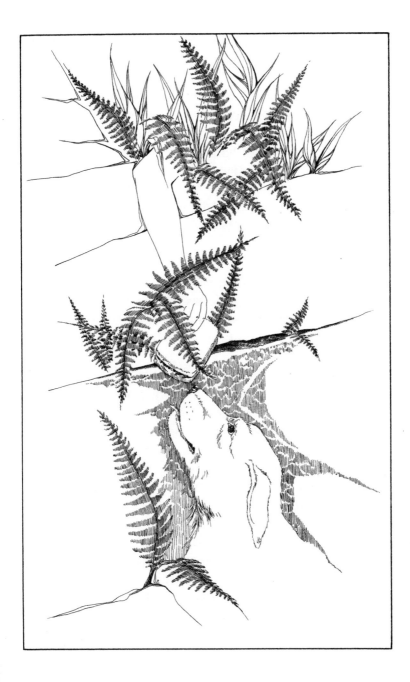

ancing along on the cut birch trunks. Once on the top of the rock, staying quiet was easy; it was covered with lichens and moss.

The hardest part was waiting. Once he had hung his arm over the edge, each minute seemed to take an hour! A yellow jacket discovered a drop of raspberry jam on his cheek, and Roz was hard-pressed to hold still when it landed on his skin and sampled the sweet-smelling treat.

Lop reached up, carefully disengaged the sandwich from the fingers, and ate it. She then smelled the fingers carefully.

They moved slowly.

Roz could not see the dog, but he began feeling her wet nose with the tips of his fingers and continued to talk in low, soothing tones. It was hard to keep calm when his blood was pumping so fast he could barely hear his own voice.

Lop was not afraid.

She stood up and sniffed from the fingers, up through the ferns past the wrist, all the way to the elbow. When Roz felt her nose was as high as the dog could reach, he slowly moved his face over the edge of the rock.

"Hello there, puppy." This time he spoke at normal volume, but in as low a tone as he could muster, and began to stroke the side of her face.

Lop was in no way intimidated. It almost seemed as if both boy and dog wanted to have more, get closer, but each was afraid the other might flee.

Head against hand, wet nose searching for more, tongue nearly washing the boy's bare arm, Lop had an emotion take hold, similar to the one she had as an orphan when she first slept between the puppies of Fox.

She stood on her hind legs, front feet bracing against the rock, and gave Roz a big, sloppy lick on the cheek. It was particularly satisfying, for she cleaned off the jam that the yellow jacket had left behind.

There was no question now of her being afraid, so Roz eased carefully over the edge and lowered himself to the ledge. It was hard to balance on the narrow strip, so dog and boy jumped to the ground, and continued to renew what had started so many months before.

Chapter Thirteen

"What now, puppy?" Roz was thinking of his father's earlier insistence that they not have a dog because of his mom's allergy. They had talked about it since. A lot. Not too many days went by without the subject coming up, and Roz began to get the feeling that his mom wouldn't mind having a dog, if it was an outdoor dog.

"A lot of people have outdoor dogs, Dad." His brain was working at warp speed again.

"Look at the Prestwicks. Remember? The coyotes got into their sheep, and they got that white dog to live with the flock?" Roz knew that was a super beginning, because they had lost several of their own lambs to coyotes, too.

"And the Byers, too, remember?" Roz was really cruising now. "Remember? Remember when their big German shepherd killed that dog-coyote when it went for their pig?"

Dan did remember. And he'd really have liked to have a dog, too.

Roz's mother usually didn't say too much when tricky

discussions were in the air, at least when Roz was in the room. She and Dan rarely disagreed in front of the boy. But . . .

"Dan, listen"—she put her hand on his arm—"listen. I know you've been protective of me, and I know it would be impossible to have a dog in the house. But I don't see how it could hurt to have a real farm dog, outside."

Roz heard it. He heard it. He did.

"Golly, honey, I don't know. It would have to have an awful thick coat. I've seen too many dogs suffer outdoors when it's cold. Makes me think some people ought to be shot, or at least chained out in the cold for a while without any clothes!"

Anyway, Roz knew the possibility was there. It might come true if he handled it right.

With his arm around Lop, he fished the baling twine out of his pocket. Always thinking, he had removed it from the saw, just in case.

He put it carefully around her neck, and secured it with a bowline knot.

When Lop felt the pressure, her first reaction was to pull back and get free. She had been tied too long not to remember and hate the feel of being trapped.

Roz felt the tenseness within the dog, and was careful to keep some slack in the string, all the while talking to her in as soothing a voice as he could muster.

He stood, coaxed her to her feet, and very slowly he and Lop walked to where he had left his knapsack and saw. Whenever she hesitated, he stopped and talked to her again, and when he took another step, she did, too.

Roz took the crackers from his knapsack, folded the little saw and put it in, then shouldered the sack and fed

Lop half a cracker. He wanted to make sure he had enough treats, in case she got balky on the way home.

His father was in town, but the boy thought it best to approach the barn on the opposite side from the house. He intended to introduce the dog to the barn animals before his father or mother knew she was there. He figured it would work better that way.

"C'mon, you old lop-eared puppy," he said softly. Together they walked down the trail to the woods road, but instead of going through the orchard, Roz led her along an old stone wall that rambled through the pine woods behind the house.

Lop followed closely, never letting the string become taut. Once past the house and the barn Roz climbed over the low stone wall. The dog hesitated, but he took half a cracker from his shirt pocket and lured her across.

At first she followed, partly to keep pressure off her neck, and partly to be with the boy. But by the time they got to the barn, the string was all but forgotten. Now she simply followed him because he represented the only gentleness she had known since being smoked out of Fox's den. These two were of like heart, and often it is a so-called lower animal who recognizes such things first.

Once in the barn Roz first led the dog down the center aisle. Two of the barn cats were warming themselves in a patch of sunlight that flowed onto the floor through a window on the south wall. When they saw the dog they simply glared at her as the boy led her by. Those cats weren't really afraid of anything.

Next they went through the sheep pens. They were all empty, for after lambing in late winter the sheep were there only at night. They didn't used to be, but since everyone was more wary of coyotes now, they kept their smaller stock inside at night.

They went through the sheep pens and out to the pigs, who weren't afraid of anything either. When Roz led Lop to the fence, an old sow plodded right over and stuck her snout between the boards. She probably weighed six hundred pounds—she was the biggest breathing thing the puppy had ever seen, or smelled! Following close behind were seven little piglets, each of which stuck its whole head through the space, the better to see. They all seemed to have a smile on their faces as they struggled to get a good look at the yellow-haired dog.

Lop licked one across the snout. Its skin tasted clean and sweet.

Next came the horses and cows. Roz and the dog went into the barnyard where he had first seen Fox's tracks. She followed him closely between two horses, and they hardly paid attention. They were old, and had seen many dogs over the years. One cow was more curious than the others, and she ambled over and smelled Lop up and down, over and across, all the while chewing her cud. Lop thought that smelled sweet, as well, whatever it was.

Introductions over, Roz was brought back to reality by thoughts of what his father would say, and he got butterflies just thinking of it. But what he had done, was done. Nothing for it now but to carry on.

He led Lop back into the barn and to a lambing pen that was farthest away from where the sheep fed at night, removed the twine from her neck, and shut the gate. He thought the fence was high enough to hold her. Then Roz fetched two pans. He filled one with water and the other with cat kibbles, and set both in the puppy's pan.

By the time he had returned, Lop had investigated the

pen, much the way she had before, when shut in the horse stall. This one had thicker straw on the floor, and the only animal she could smell was sheep.

Roz sat with the dog while she sampled the cat food. He knew full well that it was a meager meal and that it probably didn't have the right stuff in it for a dog. He got butterflies in his stomach again when he thought all this might not work out, and tried not to think about it!

Presently he heard his father's truck coming up the lane, and the butterflies almost choked off his wind.

He jumped the sheep pen fence and ran to the front of the barn.

"Hey, Dad!" His heart was in his throat.

"Hi, Rozzy. What're you doing home so soon? Havin' trouble with that wood?" Dan kind of suspected Roz's eye for a profit might have been a little stronger than his sawing arm. He successfully squelched a smile.

"No. Heck no!" Roz wanted to keep the conversation going. "Heck no. I counted the trees, figured how many pieces I could get out of each tree, but you've got to help me do some figuring. Hey, want some help with those packages?" He picked up one heavy bag of groceries and turned hopefully toward the house.

Much to the boy's relief, Dan picked up the two others and followed him, away from the barn.

For the next two days, Roz offered to feed the sheep. It didn't make much difference who did what chores. They often traded off. Each time they went to the barn Roz prayed the dog wouldn't make any noise!

She didn't.

"Mary, where's that can of hash I was saving?" Dan had particularly looked forward to having that with a couple of fried eggs on it for lunch.

"Don't know, honey. Here, let me see." She kneeled down by the counter that had the lazy Susan under it and turned it absentmindedly. "I think there's two cans of tuna missing, too. Did you have 'em?"

Dan said he hadn't. At first Mary thought Roz might have, but she had been making the lunches he took to the woods. "Have you noticed Roz being any different the last few days?"

"Sure. Listen, we figured out how much he could make this summer if I thinned out that other patch of birches back by the lake. I think he's been a little excited about that."

"Oh, Danny, don't you think that's biting off a little more than a ten year old can chew?"

"Nope. It's good for 'im. Build'm up."

Later that afternoon, when Roz came back from the woods, both his mom and dad were sitting at the kitchen table. They were watching him, as he came through the door.

There were those butterflies again! He didn't know what was up, but thought he better start talking fast.

"Hi!" He had to think fast, too. "Boy, you should see all the stuff I got cut today!" Then he went on to describe the heat and the number of frogs he had seen, and told them that a porcupine had walked right across in front of him while he was sawing.

His mom and dad glanced at each other during Roz's

monologue, but everything went okay after that, except that he couldn't find any canned meat in the cupboard for the dog. When he fed her that night it was just the old, dried cat stuff.

During the days he had taken her out to the woods for runs. He really wasn't getting much wood cut, and he knew his dad would find out eventually. He also did not like keeping secrets from his parents. It wasn't in his nature to be devious. Never had been.

That night, just after Roz had taken his bath and gotten into his pajamas, he heard thunking sounds coming from the barn. The horses were in, and they were moving nervously around on the wooden floor of their stalls.

He heard his mom call downstairs. "Dan . . . oh Dan."

Dan couldn't hear her over the sound of the radio, so Mary went downstairs. Roz followed close behind. He started to get nervous about the dog. Jig's up, jig's up, was all he could think.

"Dan, honey, maybe you ought to check the barn. The horses don't sound right."

Roz's heart fell right down through his toes!

The four went outside: Dan, Mary, Roz, and Roz's pounding heart. Halfway to the barn they heard the frightened bleating of several sheep. "Oh please, oh God, please." Roz prayed that Lop hadn't done anything bad. The boy had all his fingers crossed.

Back through the center aisle they went, and as they passed through the area of sheep pens a very clear, loud, raspy growl ripped through the air.

Dan flicked on his flashlight and stepped into the outer part of the barn.

The pigs were at full attention, facing the door to the barnyard.

Huddled in the corner, where the pig fence connected to the inner barn wall, was an old ewe. She was standing over a totally unexpected, wet, newborn lamb.

The ominous growl sounded again! Dan regretted not at least bringing a pick handle or pitchfork.

He quickly turned the light toward the sound—and there was Lop! She stood squarely in the center of the barnyard door, head lowered, her one erect ear laid back flat. She paid no attention to those behind her, and sent forth another chilling growl.

Dan walked cautiously up behind her and shined the light into the dark beyond; the beam was met by three sets of glowing eyes. Three coyotes. And when they turned, he could see that one had only half an ear.

He picked up a rock, threw it at the fading shapes, and they quickly dissolved into darkness.

Roz had his arms around the yellow dog's neck, waiting, waiting for whatever was to come. He was ready to plead, to argue, to cry, but in the end to take his medicine like a man.

"Dad, Dad, it's the puppy we got from the old fox den." His eyes filled a bit. He was prepared for the worst.

Mary put her hand gently on his father's arm.

Dan looked at his boy, and hesitated a moment before he spoke. "Son, maybe we ought to have a little talk, just maybe there are a few gaps you'd like to fill us in on . . ."

The corners of his mouth tried to curve into a smile, but he suppressed the urge.

Roz's mother did smile a tiny bit.

Dan glanced from the dog to his son, then at Mary,

and drew in a long, quiet breath. "Well, Rozzy, looks like we've got us a dog." He put his hand gently on the boy's shoulder.

"Guess we do."

Lop didn't know what all the talk was about, but her heart told her it was good.